Carolina Twilight

Carolina Twilight

A NOVEL BY
KAREN STOKES

GREEN ALTAR BOOKS
Columbia, South Carolina

CAROLINA TWILIGHT
Copyright © 2020 Karen Stokes

Published by Green Altar Books, an imprint of

Shotwell Publishing LLC
Post Office Box 2592
Columbia, South Carolina 29202

Cover image is "Carolina Twilight" by Karen Stokes
Cover design by Hazel's Dream | Boo Jackson TCB
Interior design by Dawn Silber

FIRST EDITION

ISBN: 978-1-947660-29-8

To those who sorrow without hope

Chapter One

Before leaving the house, Elaine placed a note for her parents under her pillow — a final farewell and apology.

That autumn evening in 1973, the air was still warm as the sun began to set in the Georgia sky, and she rolled down the window in her car to catch a breeze as she drove out a gravel driveway and turned onto Harrison Road. No other cars were in sight — as usual there was little traffic in this rural area, a countryside of rolling hills where scattered houses and farms were separated by acres and miles of pasture and woodlands.

She headed for the junction of the main road, which wasn't far. The intersection was at the top of a broad hill, a good place to look out on a sloping expanse of woods and watch the sun go down behind the farthest trees. Elaine had often come here to do just that, and as she pulled up to the stop sign, another glorious sunset came into view. Three columns of purplish gray clouds spanned up into the sky like the spokes of a wheel, narrowing toward the horizon, where the sun's fiery disc, the hub of that wheel, was sunken almost out of sight. Down close to the sun, against a glowing orange sky, the tapering extremity of each cloud ended in a wavy smear as though finger painted, and near it, higher in a pale salmon sky, the evening star burned — solitary and minute — but brilliant as a flare.

Waiting for a single passing car, Elaine observed all this unmoved, thinking only of her destination. Beginning her right turn, she glanced down at a letter which lay on the front seat beside her. She had taken it from the mailbox earlier that day, but it remained unopened. Her cousin Ned's letters were always funny and cheering, and she didn't want to read or think of anything that might make her have second thoughts about the grim mission she was on that evening.

About a half hour later she reached the dirt road that would take her to her family's summer cabin on the backwaters of the Chattahoochee River. Driving slowly, she wound along the red clay ruts and arrived at the driveway in less than ten minutes. As her car turned in, the headlights briefly illuminated a small rustic sign displaying the family name, *Perdreau*, and then the gray weathered siding of the cabin. Surrounded by woods, the old split level house sat at the top of a low bluff overlooking a murky inlet.

She parked the car in an area that couldn't be seen from the road. By now it was almost dark, and Elaine took a flashlight with her to unlock the front door. Entering a small foyer, she walked into a long, narrow kitchen, switched on a fluorescent lamp, and placed herself in front of a vintage gas stove. After a brief hesitation, she opened its door and turned on the gas. Kneeling and pulling her long brown hair out of the way, she put her head inside — but instantly a sudden fear came over her like a wave of nausea.

What if death was something worse than life?

She was trembling as she pulled her head out. The smell of gas had become strong.

No, she thought, I have to go through with this. I can't stand it anymore.

Swallowing hard, she put her head back inside, took a deep breath, and exhaled slowly in a sigh. Trying to keep up her courage, she asked herself if there couldn't be another possibility, that of something good and comforting on the other side. Maybe, she thought, if there was some existence after death, it was something better than life. She remembered seeing a television program about a man who had died, or nearly died, and then came back to life. He had seen a bright, beautiful light, and went to a place where there was no pain, only peace. Could it be true?

She would soon know. She listened to the faint hissing sound of the stove and made herself breathe deeply. Soon, Elaine felt herself losing consciousness. It wasn't so bad — like falling asleep. But it was a fitful sleep at first; it seemed to come and go, as though her body were fighting it. Feeling weak, she sank lower on her knees, and her head was drawn a little farther away from the oven chamber. When she opened her eyes, she could see into the shadowy sunken dining room off the kitchen, looking over the dim outlines of the tops of ladder back chairs to a window that faced the parking area in the side yard. This room was partly below ground level, and though the window was somewhat high on the wall, it was only a few feet above the driveway outside.

Her eyelids grew heavy; she had to close them again. The hissing of the gas grew louder and soon took on a mysterious rumbling sound.

Then something strange happened. Although her eyes were shut, Elaine became aware of an intense light in her face. Her eyelids fluttered open a little, and through the distortion of her eyelashes and her drowsiness, she perceived a brilliant white light.

It seemed to draw nearer and grow larger.

So it was true, she thought. Yes, the light was coming for her!

A brief, feeble sigh escaped her. Although the illumination became blindingly bright, she kept her half-open eyes on it longingly, when it suddenly stopped and came no closer.

Outside, in the driveway, a truck pulled up and parked, and someone got out. The dazzling light was merely the one working headlight on the rusty old pickup truck of her brother's best friend, who was known to use the family's cabin without permission.

She heard the car door creaking open. The light disappeared abruptly, and the last thing she remembered was trying to smile at this last, very funny joke on her.

*   *   *   *   *   *

When Elaine regained consciousness, she found herself in a hospital bed. Had she been able to cry, she would have, but feeling numb both physically and emotionally, she could only frown. Of all the possible hereafters to which she might have awakened, this was the one she considered the worst: she was still alive.

She was seventeen.

Chapter Two

Upon the recommendation of the family doctor, Elaine's parents sent her to Briarwood, the only private psychiatric hospital in the nearby city of Columbus. Walking through its entrance that first day, she felt something like a prisoner being led into a jail—but to her surprise, she soon discovered that the place was really not so bad. Despite the security monitors and the electronic locks on doors, Briarwood was not prison-like or even unpleasant in itself. Its residents enjoyed a gym, a tennis court, and even an indoor swimming pool.

Elaine met other teens with drug and "adjustment" problems, men and women of middle age recovering from alcoholism and nervous breakdowns, young housewives with phobias and other problems, and not a few patients of varying ages who, like her, were suffering from depression.

Her mealtimes were at set hours in the cafeteria, and her days were planned for her in various classes and activities. She participated in volleyball games, went swimming, and played pool at the billiard tables in the recreation room. Once or twice a week the counselors would take the teenagers and younger patients on a short walk to a city park for softball games.

She saw her therapist Dr. Jamison for an hour each weekday. Ashamed of her weakness and helplessness, especially with a stranger, Elaine was uncommunicative at first, but eventually, finding the psychiatrist sympathetic and kind, she began to answer his questions, and he pieced together her story.

When she was twelve years old, her family left the suburbs of Charleston, South Carolina, and moved to Georgia, where her father, an English professor, had secured a position at the local college in Columbus. Tired of suburbia, he purchased a new house and several acres of land in a sparsely developed, still rural area which was outside the city limits but only a short commute to the college because of a nearby interstate highway. Elaine's mother immediately found a full-time job downtown as a bookkeeper.

During that first summer in Georgia, especially after her older brother Glen found a friend in the neighborhood, Elaine was alone much of the time. Torn away from her childhood home and everyone and everything she had known and loved there, she felt strangely fragile and bewildered. To distract herself, she spent her days exploring her new environment, wandering along the country roads and in the woods with her cocker spaniel Molly, tracing creeks and investigating abandoned shanties. She had always been a great reader, and had aspirations of becoming a writer like her father, but now she read more voraciously than ever, mostly books from his library, an eclectic mixture of classic literature and modern philosophical works, perusing them with increasing desperation as she looked for answers to her mystification and pain.

Her father had published some short stories and articles, but was secretive and dissatisfied about a larger opus he had been working on for years, something dark and brooding about his military service in Korea. After the move to Columbus, it seemed to Elaine that he wrote less and drank more heavily. It became his routine each evening after supper to sit down in the den in front of the television and drink wine or liquor until he fell asleep.

Elaine's mother was so tired when she came home from work that she had no need for such a sleep aid. After preparing a meal and cleaning up afterwards, she read a book or magazine for a while in the living room, and then usually went to bed early. She argued with her husband frequently, mainly about his drinking, but tried to hide these fights from her children.

After school began in the fall, Elaine didn't tell her parents how unhappy she was at her junior high, a place where she was a complete unknown among girls and boys who had been together since kindergarten, or who knew each other from the same neighborhoods in town. She didn't tell them how an uncharacteristic shyness now fettered her in this new and unfamiliar world, and how she suffered for it in obscurity, and they didn't know that she had made only one friend— another shy girl named Marion who shared the long bus ride home with Elaine each day to the outer parts of the county. A terrible despondency took hold in her and grew worse with each passing day and month.

Whenever possible, on clear nights, while her parents read or watched television, she would climb up to the roof of the house and lie down on the shingles to observe a starry sky unobscured by city lights. Under the endless black dome and its shimmering pinpoints of diamonds, she would pick out the Pleiades, Orion and other constellations, and sometimes catch sight of the momentary streak of a falling star. Time after time, something drew her to the silent beauty of the night sky, as though she were waiting for something

Karen Stokes

from it. In her bed most nights, she soothed herself with fantasies of a lover—a man, handsome and strong, who would save her from her loneliness and misery.

After junior high, Elaine's unhappiness worsened when she was assigned to a different high school than Marion. Her parents thought this pronounced sadness was a phase of adolescent moodiness, and waited for it to pass. Glen had gone through his own phase of moodiness and rebellion, after all, and yet he had turned out all right, and would soon be studying engineering at Georgia Tech in Atlanta. They didn't consider, however, that Glen was much more outgoing and confident than his sister, gifted in sports, and somehow able to make all A's without a stigma. Extremely good looking and well groomed, he had been popular in high school, though a newcomer his first year. Their shy daughter, on the other hand, dressed herself in a drab hippie fashion, wore too much makeup to hide her blemishes, was inept in physical education classes, and received only resentment from other students when she effortlessly made the honor roll every term. Elaine couldn't do otherwise with her grades; it was a kind of compulsion with her. Her parents seemed to be proud of her as a student, if nothing else.

During her second summer in Georgia, as a sort of consolation prize for taking her away from Charleston, Elaine's parents gave her riding lessons and purchased a horse for her, a palomino quarter horse mare named Cherry. Part of the lot was cleared and fenced off with barbed wire for a paddock, and Glen helped his father build a small stable with one stall and a storage room for tack.

Seated on a shiny new English saddle, Elaine went out riding as often as she could. On hot summer days she would ride to some rolling pastureland a few miles away. Cherry knew where to go, and took her to a shady spot beside a creek. She let the horse graze nearby while she rested on the grassy bank, looking up at armadas of white, flat-bottomed clouds moving slowly across the sky toward the west. Elaine wondered where the cloud-ships were going, often wishing she could merely dwindle into oblivion and be blown away like the mists of nothingness above her — like a ghost.

When she was old enough to get a driver's license, her parents bought her a used automobile — but despite the car, the horse, and any number of other comforts and luxuries they provided for her, Elaine's unhappiness and insecurity only continued to deepen as she grew older. By the time she finished high school (a year earlier than her classmates) her depression was almost incapacitating. Marion, her only real friend, had acquired a boyfriend during her third year in high school and was spending spend less time with her. In desperation, Elaine couldn't imagine what to do with her life. The thought of college was extremely intimidating, and yet it was expected of her to attend the school where her father taught.

The closer the day of registration at college drew, the more withdrawn and anguished she became. Sleep had been difficult for her before — now it was almost impossible. Suicide had crossed her mind frequently in the past, but now she seriously began to contemplate the method. Knowing that she didn't have the physical courage to face a form of death which was not quick or painless, she rejected numerous ideas. She thought of turning on the car in the closed garage, but realized that she might not have time to carry this out, as her father sometimes came home for lunch, or at odd hours during the day between classes. The idea of painless fumes, though, appealed to her as the easiest way to go, and it was then she remembered the gas stove at their cabin on the river.

A feeling of relief swept over her. Finally, there was a way out.

She wrote several versions of a suicide note before settling on the precise wording, checked with her best friend to make sure she would be busy that particular evening, and told her parents that she would be spending the night at Marion's house. The next morning, she woke up in the hospital.

*   *   *   *   *   *

After a month passed at Briarwood with no sign of improvement in Elaine, Dr. Jamison put her on antidepressants and tranquilizers. Though they made her feel a little better, they had their drawbacks. The medications caused her blood pressure to drop, and gave her constant heartburn and headaches. Eventually the heartburn went away, and the headaches decreased, but the low blood pressure remained. If she stood up too quickly, she began to black out.

Once, while alone in the music room, she fainted as she got up from a chair to change a record on a stereo. One moment she was reaching for a replay button, and the next, falling to the floor as a thousand spots of blackness coalesced before her eyes. As she hit the carpet she felt the impact, but no pain, and when she came around, still alone in the music room, she heard her James Taylor album playing. It was a song she listened to frequently, about a girl who had killed herself.

The other teenagers at Briarwood, many of whom were there for drug abuse problems, were temperamental but friendly. There was an odd kind of camaraderie among almost all the patients that Elaine had never experienced. One highly intelligent, nerdish boy named Donald was drawn to Elaine, and finding that she was kind and never teased him, he sometimes sat with her at meals and talked about books and movies, and filled her in on things he thought she ought to know about getting along at Briarwood.

One evening at dinner she asked Donald why he was in the hospital. He told her he was schizophrenic.

"You seem all right to me," she responded, surprised.

"That's because I'm taking lots of medication. Without it, you would find me extremely weird."

Donald laughed, making nervous, twitching movements with his shoulders and hands. He did have an odd manner, and seldom looked her in the eye, but she would never have taken him for a person with such a serious disorder.

"You don't seem out of touch with reality," she remarked.

"Oh, you wouldn't believe what's gone on in my head. You wouldn't believe it."

"Like what?"

"Well…"

He hesitated, shrugging.

"Voices in my head told me to read *Mein Kampf*, and they said I should like Hitler."

Elaine was somewhat shocked, but said, "I don't believe that."

"But it's true. I told you I was sick."

"Then that was your sickness, not you. You don't hear voices telling you things like that now, do you?"

"No, I don't," Donald whispered, hanging his head.

"You're nice," he added, glancing into her eyes only momentarily.

Elaine admired a red-haired, pale girl who always wore long skirts and stylish boots. Her face was delicately beautiful, her figure exquisite. She was soft-spoken, reserved, and rarely smiled. Elaine didn't get to know her very well, but heard that she was in the hospital because she had lost her fiancé in an automobile accident.

The red-haired girl and an older man were inseparable. His name was Robert. He was perhaps in his fifties, and was at Briarwood for alcoholism. He was extremely thin, with a complexion both ruddy and pale, a narrow Nordic face, watery blue eyes, sandy hair, and a swollen red nose. His reddish beard was clipped closely to his face. He smoked with a short cigarette holder, and was usually badly dressed in polyester leisure suits or gauzy short-sleeved shirts. His voice was soft and quavering, and sometimes, when amused, he had a distinctive way of sucking the air in through his teeth and releasing a weak, throaty laugh.

The red-haired girl and Robert were always seen together, sometimes sitting on a couch in the day-room with his head on her shoulder. He had apparently won the young woman's confidence by simple persistence, and by showing himself harmless and devoted. He complimented her constantly, but was sincere, and seemed to appreciate her gentleness and sensitivity. In return she consoled and befriended him.

Robert preferred to worry about the girl and her welfare rather than his own, though he was sometimes dejected about himself. He liked Elaine because she was also shy and quiet, but he never divided his attentions, and stuck close to his lovely, gentle friend, especially when she was preparing to leave the hospital to return to her family in Texas. The two had a tearful parting, but after she was gone Robert was in a particularly good mood for a few days. Perhaps he was happy for her. Afterwards, he spent more time with the adults his own age, but once, after returning to the hospital from a weekend pass, he was seen sitting in a chair with his face turned into the cushion. After this episode he sought out Elaine's company. One afternoon he sat down beside her on the day-room couch and asked if he could put his head on her shoulder. She let him. He told her that his wife was going to leave him. Elaine felt sorry for him and talked with him for a while.

When Robert learned that Elaine liked to write poems and stories, he told her about the books he had been reading, works on philosophy and political matters. He said that he was making notes from his reading and working on his own book about world peace. His plan to accomplish peace in the world was to institute a program of exchange for citizens of different nations, including the displacement of entire communities. For instance, he explained, an individual or family from the Soviet Union would come to live in United States for a period, and an equal number of Americans would in turn go to the U.S.S.R., and so on, with every country and people on earth. This plan, he felt, would eradicate prejudice and bring about understanding, and do away with war, which was caused by ignorance and fear. It was his opinion that people should live their lives according to the tenets of the Sermon on the Mount, and other Christian principles, excepting those restrictions on sexual relations. He felt those restrictions would be unacceptable to most people, and perhaps cause them to reject his program altogether. He wanted to abolish marriage, except for those who wished to remain monogamous by mutual consent. He had his doubts as to whether men were meant to be monogamous. He thought people were bad because of their upbringing or environment, and that if external conditions were corrected, a utopia would result. He was very worried about nuclear war.

His wife, he said, thought he was a crazy dreamer, out of touch with reality, and she scorned his book writing. She sounded sensible, if blunt and cruel. It appeared to Elaine that she merely wished him to worry about his own problems (and his family's) rather than those of the world. He did seem barely able to take care of himself.

Robert asked Elaine what she thought of his ideas. She hated to lie to him because she sensed that some people had been lying to him a great deal, telling him that he was distraught for very noble reasons. Perhaps that was really the case, but it seemed to her that he was using world problems as a diversion from his own deep troubles. He was pathetic, and looked it, and all the more because he gave the impression that, deep inside, he knew himself to be pathetic, but could not let himself realize it. And yet he believed himself a lover of truth.

He seemed unaware that most of his ideas were not original, and did not realize how uneducated he was. He was reading Shakespeare for the first time in his life. He asked Elaine about her writing and got her to talk a little about it, but as she spoke about her poems and stories, she felt rather pathetic herself, and wondered if she was as absurd in her aspirations as Robert was.

*   *   *   *   *   *

One Saturday night, Donald came back to Briarwood early from a weekend pass at home looking deeply agitated. Elaine was nearby when his parents brought him in, and she could hear him screaming at them in anger. A brawny male orderly escorted him to his room and locked him inside. The next morning, Donald seemed calm, though more withdrawn than usual. At lunch and dinner he sat alone, ate little, and then, sometime after the evening meal, he managed to leave the building undetected. He wasn't missed until the nighttime medications were being handed out at the nurse's station.

The staff questioned all the patients about the last time they had seen Donald. The head doctor was called in, and he notified Donald's parents and the police that he was missing.

"The freak's run away to join the circus," chuckled one teenage boy who liked to insult and torment Donald.

Glaring at him, Elaine left the commotion in that part of the building for the solitude of the library, a quiet little place off one of the hallways.

The hospital's random collection of reading material had few things that interested her except for a few classic novels, her usual fare. She had spent most of her free time reading *Gone with the Wind*, a book she fairly devoured. Now she was reading *Madame Bovary*, and was on the last few chapters. By the time Elaine finished the novel things had quieted down in the hospital, and she went to her room to go to bed.

The next morning, after breakfast, the usual routine at Briarwood was interrupted for a special meeting in the arts and crafts room. All the patients came in and took a seat at long tables arranged in a large square. The head physician was already seated, along with several counselors and a nurse. When everyone was settled and quiet, he announced that the meeting concerned Donald. Speaking slowly and somberly, he explained that the teenager had been found. Donald had broken into the chemistry lab of a nearby high school, found a toxic substance, and consumed it. He was still alive when a janitor found him in the early morning, but died shortly after arriving at the emergency room.

Elaine began to weep as she heard the news, and a counselor came to her side and put his arm around her shoulder. Some of the other patients were wiping away tears and shaking their heads in disbelief and sorrow. The head doctor looked deathly pale, but kept his professional demeanor.

Although deeply grieved, Elaine felt awkward about her outburst and took a deep breath to regain her composure. When the meeting was over she got permission to go back to her room and skip all the morning activities.

Alone in her bed, she could not help but weep again for this poor, sick, agonized boy. He had eaten arsenic, like Emma Bovary.

Chapter Three

During her seventh week at Briarwood, Dr. Jamison scheduled a "family conference." Elaine's brother Glen wasn't able to be there, but her parents showed up promptly. Her father was very cooperative and made a sincere effort to understand his daughter's depression. He was astounded to learn that, as Dr. Jamison contended, Elaine felt unloved.

"I really can't see how she could feel that way," said Dr. Perdreau, looking helplessly to Dr. Jamison, then to Elaine, who sat expressionless and silent. Distraught, Mrs. Perdreau blamed herself, but without sincerity.

"I must be a terrible mother," she cried tearfully. "I must be a terrible person."

The session lasted for an hour. Elaine noticed all her father's uneasy postures and nervous looks. This probably wasn't what he had expected at all, she thought, feeling a little sorry for him and her mother, since she didn't blame them for her unhappiness. After all, it wasn't their fault that she was defective and unlovely; she simply ought never to have been born.

Only Dr. Perdreau came to the next family conference. He swore that he would quit drinking, thinking that it was his alcoholism which had distressed his daughter so much, and it wasn't long after this session that Elaine actually seemed to start getting better, but only because the antidepressants and tranquilizers were finally taking full effect. She slept better, and found it easier not to brood constantly about herself. She was able to live in and think of only the present moment, avoiding the feelings of dread and despair that thoughts of the future brought. She knew the drugs were a false peace, but enjoyed the numbness anyway. Emotionally exhausted by her agonies, she allowed herself to drift along in a kind of drug-induced apathy. Nothing moved her much, but nothing hurt her much, either.

One day in mid-December she told Dr. Jamison that she wanted to go home, and was ready for it. He agreed. About a week and a half afterward, just before Christmas, Elaine was discharged from the hospital.

The Perdreaus were relieved to have their daughter home again. As far as they could tell she was getting better — the crisis seemed to be over. They had not told Elaine's grandmother or any other relatives or friends in Charleston about her crisis, and before long, Elaine's mother began to act as if there never had been one. Her father was gentler with her and more attentive. He was drinking less, but didn't give it up altogether.

The winter term at the college began in early January. Elaine was still intimidated by the prospect, and knew in her heart that things would be disastrous for her there. Nevertheless, on a certain morning, she got into her car, drove to the college, and registered as a student. Fortified with her courage in capsule form, she didn't find the experience as painful and difficult as she thought it would be. Still, as she moved about in the crowded confusion of registration day, her anxieties about the unfamiliar procedure were replaced by other troubling concerns. Apart from a few faculty members who were personal friends of her father, she didn't know a soul on campus. All the teenagers who had been her classmates were still in their senior year of high school. She felt very much alone in the crowds, and out of place, possibly the only seventeen-year-old among them.

For the first term Elaine signed up for three required courses. She made a few acquaintances, but no real friends. She was quiet and inconspicuous in her classes, and never stayed on campus a moment longer than necessary. Two days a week she lunched with her father in the cafeteria. The other three days, he taught a class during her free hour. Then Elaine would eat alone, if she ate at all, and that outside if the weather was tolerable. Some boys noticed her, but she gave them no encouragement. She finished the winter term with high grades in all her courses.

The spring break was like an oasis in a desert for her. She spent lots of time with Marion, who had broken up with her boyfriend. Both girls shared a newfound interest in photography, and they walked or drove to interesting places in the area to take pictures. In the evenings at Marion's house, they watched television or danced to records, and laughed and groaned over their old "man-crazy" scrapbooks from junior high, filled with pictures of actors and pop stars.

Elaine continued to see Dr. Jamison once a week. He thought she was making good progress, but was unaware that his patient wasn't always completely honest with him. In her inmost self, she felt that nothing had changed for her; that she was only artificially keeping despair at bay, and that one day, perhaps soon, it would swallow her up again.

In the spring term she continued with more required courses, but also signed up for an elective that interested her. It was an art history class which concentrated on ancient Greek, Roman, and Byzantine cultures, subjects she was already familiar with from books she had read on archaeology. For this course she expected to have as instructor one Mr. Myers—a portly, middle-aged man she knew by sight—but on the first day of class the head of the department came in and announced that a Mr. Reese would teach the course instead; he told the students what textbook to buy and dismissed them.

As Elaine walked into the fine arts building the next day she noticed a young man, unmistakably a teacher, whom she had never seen before. He was ahead of her on the stairs to the second floor, carrying a book and papers under one arm, and walking with a confident, springing step. From only a brief glimpse of his face she could see that he was handsome. He had thick black hair, and was dressed in earth tones—faded olive corduroy jeans, and a suede jacket that was the golden buckskin color of her palomino mare.

On the second floor she paused in the hall and watched where he walked. When he went into her art classroom, she knew he must be the new instructor Mr. Reese. Elaine waited a moment and then slowly ambled in.

She happened to be the first student to arrive. As she entered the room Mr. Reese looked up from the podium where he was struggling to put on a tie. He smiled and greeted her with a "Good afternoon." To her ear his voice was without any accent, like that of a television news reporter.

For a few moments there was only the two of them in the

classroom. He managed to finish with the tie and began thumbing through some papers. As other students trickled in, Elaine studied him. He was somewhat tall, inclining to thinness, but well-proportioned. The lines of his face were elegant and lean, and yet at the same time somewhat boyish looking. Elaine guessed he was in his late twenties.

That day, class was fairly brief. Mr. Reese introduced himself (his first name was Alan), and outlined the various periods and styles of ancient art the course would cover. Like most of the instructors in this department, he was easygoing and informal, and friendly with the students. He frequently smiled and made jokes — all successful. Elaine could tell he would be popular.

Not feeling constrained by shyness in this setting, where everyone watched the teacher, she seldom took her eyes from his face — and yet the profound effect he had on her was not evident in her outward appearance, which was impassive and calm.

That day, she could almost believe there really was some quivered god of love hovering over poor mortals. When he smiled at her for the first time, it was as though a sharp, intoxicating arrow had pierced her heart. In the afternoon, Elaine left the campus preoccupied in bittersweet confusion — the taste of infatuation sweet, but the prospect of inevitable disappointment and pain, bitter indeed.

Chapter Four

In class the next day Mr. Reese was friendly as before, but a little more businesslike and earnest. The lights were turned off for a slide presentation, and he began his lecture. He stood at the podium, to one side of a large screen behind him. He spoke at a leisurely but steady pace, not often looking down at his notes. When he did look down, his straight black hair fell over one eye, and he swept it back with a quick, automatic movement of his head and hand. Elaine observed his profile, which was illuminated by the streaming light of the projector. As he reached out to point to an area on a map, her eyes went to his left hand; there was no ring on it.

Over the weekend Elaine often thought about Alan Reese, wondering what he was doing, where he lived. She went shopping for some new clothes, and chose apparel which, judging by his tastes, she thought he might like. On Sunday she went to the public library, where she happened to see him coming out of the building, walking toward the parking lot. He didn't see her at first; when he did he waved with a brisk movement, bowing his head forward in a characteristic way. She took it as a good sign that he had at least recognized her from a distance.

During the second week of class, a small incident occurred which, for Elaine, began a momentous new phase in life. Mr. Reese had paused in his lecture to answer a student's question. That done, he looked at the slide projection and began again, then hesitated as if trying to recall something, and for a few moments shuffled through his notes on the podium. On the screen behind him glowed an image of a golden mask.

"I thought I had it here," he said with mild irritation. "The man's name has slipped my mind…It'll come to me. Anyway, this is one of the pieces excavated at Mycenae—"

Before Elaine knew it she had blurted out the name.

"Schliemann," she said.

"Yes, that's it. Thank you, Elaine," said Mr. Reese.

He looked somewhat impressed, and favored her with a smile and a nod of acknowledgment, continuing, "Heinrich Schliemann, a famous German archaeologist…"

From then on, as though curious about the extent of her knowledge, he often consulted Elaine instead of his notes, and more often than not she knew the answer. Once in a while, before imparting some bit of information to the class, he would pause, smile, and question Elaine about the matter to see if she already knew it. He began to favor her for little tasks in the class instead of choosing someone at random to do them. The girl who sat in front of Elaine, one of the few students with whom she had become friendly, teased her about being "teacher's pet."

Once, Elaine had dreaded going to the college; now she lived for it. Frequently she would cut short lunch to be early for her class with Mr. Reese, though he usually arrived only minutes before the bell. One afternoon, when bad weather kept most of the other students away, and delayed almost everyone else, she was alone for him for ten minutes. He was busy with some papers, but they did talk a little—about the weather. After class Elaine often lingered in the halls, perusing exhibitions of student artwork, hoping to catch a glimpse of him. She would see him emerging from his office, or working in there, or standing in the doorway of another teacher's office, talking and smoking a cigarette. She coveted the job of the student who sometimes worked as his assistant, a tall, sweet-faced girl with long blonde hair.

Near mid-term Elaine began to notice advertisements around campus for the drama department's upcoming production. Mr. Reese was a friend of the drama professor, and mentioned one day in class that he was helping with the play. He also made it known that some volunteers were needed to assist with scenery and costumes. The following afternoon, Elaine worked up enough courage to present herself at the college theater and offer her services. They gave her the job of painting scenery.

The play was a musical, *Man of La Mancha*. Elaine often worked during the rehearsals, learning the words to all the songs she liked by heart. She didn't see Alan Reese as often as she had hoped to, but when he was there he was working near her, and would talk to her about things other than ancient art and the weather. He urged her to call him by his first name outside of class, and she gladly complied. She overheard his conversations with others, and from these gathered a little more information about him. He was twenty-nine years old, an artist as well as a teacher of art, and was neither married nor engaged. He lived alone in an apartment just off campus.

With the young women involved in the play he was merely

friendly, though there was one attractive girl with whom he seemed to flirt at times, in a joking way. Elaine disliked her intensely.

When the scenery and costumes were completed, Elaine's only opportunity to talk with the handsome teacher outside class was gone, but less than a week later another chance came her way. One day at noon, when she came into the cafeteria to have lunch with her father, she saw Dr. Perdreau sitting in the usual place—with Alan Reese.

She took her tray over to the table with a pounding heart, trying not to look excessively pleased when she greeted them.

"I was just saying, I didn't realize you were Dr. Perdreau's daughter," he remarked as Elaine sat down opposite him, "but I really should have known from the name."

"Does she get preferred treatment now, Alan?" her father asked humorously.

He smiled and replied with a languid shake of the head.

The two men resumed a conversation Elaine had interrupted about the new president of the college. She didn't really listen, since her father was doing most of the talking. Now and then Alan would glance at her. She felt that she was eating awkwardly; she couldn't taste her food. At one point Dr. Perdreau became aware that he was ignoring his daughter. He paused to ask her if she had finished her paper on Thomas Hardy.

"Almost," she answered.

Alan gazed at her with interest.

"Hardy's tales are rather bleak, aren't they?" he asked her.

Literature was her great love, and she replied with a sudden earnestness which immediately embarrassed her.

"But beautiful," said Elaine.

Alan nodded thoughtfully.

"I'm sure you know better than I," he answered graciously.

Dr. Perdreau began to talk about the college play, embarrassing Elaine again by telling Alan how she had raved about his set designs. He dealt with the compliments by returning some of his own for her.

"Couldn't have done it without our hardworking volunteers," he said, smiling at her warmly. "Elaine's very talented. She was a big help. I'm very proud of my only recruit."

Dr. Perdreau put his arm around her shoulders.

"I've always said that Elaine was capable of doing anything she wanted to."

His indulgent, somewhat condescending manner made her feel childish.

"I'm sure she is," Alan agreed.

Her father kept patting her shoulder and looking expectantly at her while she tried to recover her composure.

"I just thought it would be fun to work on a play," she said. She blushed and hung her head; she had meant to say "interesting" instead of "fun," thinking it would sound more grown up.

But Alan didn't seem to find her remark childish, and even echoed her sentiment. It had been fun working on the play, but—

"Never again," he said with a laugh. "At least not this year. Too much work…speaking of which—"

He had to get back to some. Before he left, however, he reminded Dr. Perdreau about an invitation he had given earlier, and extended it to Elaine. Some of his paintings were to be exhibited in the upcoming faculty art show. They promised they would come.

When he was gone Elaine asked her father about Alan Reese, as though merely interested in him as an artist, but all that Dr. Perdreau seemed to know was that he had taught art at a college in

Atlanta before moving to Columbus.

"Alan said you were his best student," he added, while they were on the subject.

"He talked about me?" she asked, suddenly intent.

"Just before you came in I mentioned that you were in his class," said Dr. Perdreau, eyeing his daughter with a touch of puzzlement.

"Oh," she murmured. So her father had brought her up in their conversation.

"Alan and I only met recently. He merely remarked that you were his best student…that's all."

"Oh," she repeated, and then, because she thought her father was looking at her somewhat strangely, quickly added, "I was just wondering if he mentioned how I did on a test we had yesterday."

*   *   *   *   *   *

The faculty art show opened on a Sunday afternoon. Elaine had spent a good part of that morning in front of her dresser mirror doing and redoing her hair, trying to come up with a style that would make her heart-shaped face look narrower. After experimenting with a half a dozen or so various looks, fretting all the while over her ineptness with rollers and hairpins, she ended up with a style not very much different from the one she usually wore. She assessed the results with a slight frown of disappointment, but she felt better when she put on a flattering dress she had bought for today's occasion. When she was finally ready to leave she surveyed herself with moderate approval in a long mirror on the back of the door.

Both her parents came with her to the show, but when they arrived at the fine arts building she left them and went off by herself. For the opening day there was a table set up in the anteroom of the gallery. Behind the white tablecloths, and rows of petit-fours and finger sandwiches, a young woman stood ladling punch into clear plastic glasses. She was the attractive girl who had helped with the costumes for the play and sometimes flirted with Alan Reese. The sight of her discouraged Elaine.

Alan was standing near the end of the banquet table, cigarette in hand, talking with an elderly couple. Hoping that he would notice her, Elaine came closer. The young woman offered her a glass of punch, but she pretended not to notice, and picked up one from the table. While she looked over the food a young man walked up and stood beside the girl serving punch. From the intimate way they talked and leaned close to one another it was plain to Elaine that they were more than friends. She smiled to herself and took a piece of cake.

A moment later, Alan walked over to her.

"I'm glad you could come, Elaine" he said, returning her instantly broadened smile. "Is your father here?"

Elaine told him that her parents were around somewhere, noticing as she spoke that he looked rather tired. He took a drag on his cigarette and exhaled in a quick, tense sigh, then asked her what she thought about the show.

"I haven't really seen it yet," she answered apologetically.

He stared at her, or through her, for a moment, oblivious, having heard a familiar voice nearby, and in the next instant he turned toward a man who had called his name and was beckoning to him from a crowd of people in the doorway.

"Will you excuse me?"

But before Alan left he put his hand on her shoulder to point her toward the gallery.

"Go and see the show, and tell me what you think of it," he said, giving her a friendly pat on the back.

Dr. and Mrs. Perdreau were already inside the gallery, standing in front of a large painting which hung on one of the four massive pillars in the room. Elaine stayed by herself and looked for Alan's paintings. She knew that there were three in the show. She walked over to a group of paintings that hung near the gallery entrance and found them immediately. They were abstracts of riotous color and movement, and none were titled, only numbered. Elaine had always been indifferent to abstract art, and was indecisive as to whether she liked these works; they were interesting to her only because they were Alan's creations.

The rest of the reception was a disappointment for her. Alan was so busy with other guests that Elaine's parents hardly saw him long enough to say hello, and Elaine only had time to congratulate him and say goodbye.

Much to her delight, though, her father's friendship with Alan Reese led to a gradual change in their relationship, which became something a little more than teacher and student. Outside class, she always called him by his first name now, and he treated her more like a friend. During the last weeks of the term he frequently lunched with Elaine and her father, and afterwards would walk to the fine arts building with her.

Alan seemed to genuinely like her, so she allowed herself a little hope. In May she turned eighteen.

*   *   *   *   *   *

One afternoon in the last week of the term Elaine saw Alan walking out of his office with an expensive-looking camera. He stopped to speak to her.

"I didn't know you were a photographer, too," she said, admiring the camera.

"I haven't had much time for it during the past few months, but lately I've had this irresistible urge—"

He suddenly raised the camera and took a picture of her.

"Don't" she cried laughingly, too late.

"Let me take another one," he said, advancing the film. "And this time don't try to hide."

He raised the camera and focused, but soon decided that the light would be better outside. He seated her on a stone bench under a willow tree and snapped several pictures. Afterwards they talked about photography, and he learned that Elaine was something of a shutterbug herself.

On the last day of class, after all the other students were gone, Elaine asked Alan if would like to see some of her photographs. With his enthusiastic yes, she shyly placed a folder on the podium. Alan opened it and examined the pictures inside. He thought they were all good, and there was one in particular that he admired very much. He told her that she showed promise, and had a natural ability with the camera.

So much praise was unexpected. Elaine put away the folder with a pleasure as acute as her embarrassment.

"You should keep up with your picture-taking this summer," he remarked, and asked her if she was going to Florida during vacation.

"I might," she said. "Are you?"

He shook his head. He was going back to Atlanta to visit his family.

"What courses will you be teaching this summer?" she asked,

hoping to sign up for one.

"I won't be here this summer," he answered, gathering up papers as he prepared to leave.

Elaine was unable to hide her disappointment.

"So you'll be teaching your next class in the fall?"

"No, I won't be teaching here at all next year."

"Where will you teach?"

"Well, it's not certain right now. I've been asked to teach some classes at the museum, but I'm not sure I will."

His tone had become vague and evasive. In the silence that followed Elaine caught herself staring at him, and corrected a too-obvious frown. Alan's manner was decidedly cool and aloof when they said their goodbyes.

Chapter Five

Elaine had always looked forward to the summer months as a relief from the dreary burden and trial of school. Her depression usually lessened a little when she was free from it. But this year the spring had been her time of respite — because of Alan — and now summer was a return to her usual bleak and despondent state of mind. After that last day at the college it came on quickly.

There were times, usually after some extreme disappointment or humiliation, when her depression became all but intolerable. It was that way for her now, but with the added torture of love-sickness. The antidepressants and tranquilizers no longer seemed to do her much good. Her energy was low, and nothing interested her. She took long naps during the day, and at night, unable to sleep, she stayed up until dawn watching old movies for distraction. She stayed in her room most of the time with her dog, not even wishing to see her family or her best friend, and became more and more reclusive. Thoughts of death came to her again.

In June, Elaine's parents were contemplating a family vacation. Her father wanted to take a trip to the mountains of North Carolina to escape the heat; her mother wanted to go to Savannah. A trip to Savannah also meant a visit to Charleston to see Elaine's grandmother Adele and other relatives, including Ned, who was her favorite cousin and a childhood playmate. As much as Elaine loved her grandmother and Ned, however, she had no wish to see any of her relatives. After much discussion her parents settled on a compromise about the vacation. They would take short trip to the mountains now, and then a longer one to Charleston and Savannah in the fall, and perhaps even the mountains again, when the weather was more pleasant.

Elaine refused to go with them, but they were reluctant to leave her home alone. The problem was solved when Marion called and invited Elaine to drive down to Florida with her. So Elaine spent a week in Panama City with her friend, and the change of scene, the beach and the sunshine cheered her at least a little. The two girls worked on their tans and spent their evenings at the amusement parks and movie theaters.

On the last day of their vacation, Elaine woke early and went for a walk by herself on the beach. The sun was just coming up over the horizon, and except for an old lady walking a dog, she saw no one for a long while, until several teenage boys spilled out of the doorway of one of the newer motels, laughing and raucous, and dressed in swimming trunks and tee shirts. They peeled off their shirts and began diving into a swimming pool, but one slender young man with light brown hair walked to the edge of the pool area, leaned over a railing, and looked out at the ocean. When he caught sight of Elaine he smiled and craned his head forward to get a better look.

Normally such ogling would have caused her to look away immediately, but the boy looked so familiar, she couldn't take her eyes off him at first. He looked just like her cousin Ned from Charleston. Every year, her grandmother sent his school picture to Elaine's parents, and since it was always displayed on the refrigerator in a little magnetic frame, his grinning mug was an everyday sight in the household. When she realized that the boy watching her wasn't Ned, she turned away and quickened her pace to put him behind her.

The thought of her cousin caused memories of childhood to float through her mind as she continued her solitary walk, and she recalled playing in the sand with him on Sullivan's Island and Folly Beach near Charleston, and laughing at his frequent jokes and clownish antics. Life seemed so carefree then—hopeful and even happy—but despite the fact that it was only a matter of a mere decade past, the days of her childhood seemed like something from another century.

She wondered what Ned was doing for the summer, and remembered that she had never answered his last letter. Over the last winter and spring he had written to her a few times, but she didn't like to reply. Unlike him, she had nothing cheerful to report, and had no wish to disclose her misery.

Elaine and Marion spent the rest of the day sunbathing, swimming and browsing various souvenir shops. That evening they ate at a seafood restaurant and spent the last of their money on a final visit to the amusement park.

She returned home with bronzed skin and lightened hair. But the rest of the summer lay before her. Marion began a full-time job, and Elaine was even more alone than ever.

*　*　*　*　*　*

Late on one humid, overcast afternoon, Elaine went out horseback riding for the first time in weeks. The sun had been hidden all day, but not long after she left the house it finally came out from behind the scattering clouds. The brightness and heat of the day became a little uncomfortable, and she guided her horse off the main highway on to a shady rural road. There were only a few old houses along this route, along with some scattered newer homesteads on woody lots with long driveways. She rode to the end, cantering at certain open stretches, then turned around and came back down the same road. By the time she had traveled half the distance again it was becoming dusk, her favorite part of the day. She took her feet out the high stirrups of her saddle and let her boots dangle, allowing the horse to amble at the pace she chose. For once her mare didn't seem in an inordinate hurry to get home to supper.

Elaine took a detour on a path which led to a creek near the road. It made a turn here to run roughly parallel to the main highway down to a lake near her house. She and Marion used to hike its length, walking along the creek bed or on rocks in the shallow parts, and along the wooded banks where the water was turbid and deeper, a home to water moccasins. She thought it was a pretty stream, and sat down beside it to enjoy the sound of the flowing, gurgling waters.

It was beginning to turn dark when she finally went back to the shady road and continued the ride home. As her horse rounded a bend, a pasture on the far side of the road revealed an open space of sky. Here, along the horizon, a pale violet haze mingled with the clear blue sky above, creating a band of beautiful indigo color. In this haze a full moon glowed a pinkish gold in color. Elaine had paused to admire that sight, when she heard a car door slam and, for a moment, the sound of a man's voice singing or humming. Up ahead she could see another driveway. It led to a little house which sat just off the road behind a row of tall hedges. She knew the place well; a friend of her brother had rented it once, and she had been inside several times with Glen. The house had been unoccupied for a long time, but apparently it was vacant no longer.

The line of hedges was broken by the space where a rusty metal gate stood open. Elaine had just steered her horse closer to the edge of the road to avoid the gate when she saw a man take hold of it to close it. He gave it a pull and then leaned down to kick away an obstructing mound of dirt. The man looked up as she was passing by, and she recognized Alan Reese.

"Hello," she said, bringing her horse to a halt.

Alan thought he recognized the voice, and came closer to see her better in the twilight.

"Is that you, Elaine?"

He was smiling.

"Yes. Is that you?" she laughed nervously.

"What a surprise! You live near here?" he asked. There was no sign of the strange coldness of their last conversation in his tone.

"On Harrison Road—it's not far from here," she said, coughing a little. Her voice was breaking.

"I guess we'll be neighbors for a while, then."

This revelation came as music to her ears.

"You're renting this place?"

He nodded.

"Moved in today. Actually I'm not quite finished. I'm afraid I got a late start."

"Can I help you?" she asked, coughing again.

"Well, as a matter of fact, you can. I was having a little trouble getting a trunk through the back door…"

Elaine dismounted, tied her horse at the gate, and walked up the short driveway with Alan. His car had a small trailer hitched to it, and was parked in the back yard. She merely had to help him lift and maneuver an awkward trunk through the doorway. The job was over in a moment. Alan wiped his face with a handkerchief and offered her something to drink.

The light in the small kitchen didn't turn on when he flipped the switch.

"The bulb must be burnt out," he muttered.

In the semi-darkness Elaine felt her way across the room and flipped another switch. The naked light bulb in the ceiling flashed on.

"The wiring in this house is kind of crazy," she explained. "You have to have this switch on or the other won't turn on or off."

"How did you know that?" he asked, surprised.

"My brother's friend used to rent this place. Glen brought me here a few times when he had to babysit me."

"Great! If I have any other problems here I'll just call on you," he said jokingly, taking a bottle of ice water out of an otherwise empty refrigerator.

"I'm afraid water is all I have right now, until I can get some groceries."

As Elaine watched him pour out two glasses of water she was overwhelmingly conscious of the stillness and quiet of the house, and their isolation and aloneness here—an isolation made more complete by the fall of night.

"Are you living here by yourself?" she asked him.

"Yep, just me and my shadow."

He handed her a glass and drank his own down thirstily.

After a sip she asked him why he had picked this lonely place. Alan finished his drink before he answered.

"That's—a little complicated." His tone was politely evasive. "Let's just say I wanted to get away from it all for a while."

Elaine nodded as though she understood.

"I didn't tell many people where I would be," he went on. "I want it that way so that I can get some work done this summer without a lot of interruptions. I'm not even going to have a phone..."

Elated by the mere sight of him, Elaine only half-listened, hardly able to believe her good luck. The kitchen window was open, and she heard her horse impatiently snorting and stamping outside. She took a look out the window, but couldn't quite see her mare Cherry. When she turned back to Alan he was studying her with a faint smile.

"Do you often go riding at night?" he asked, leaning against the kitchen counter with crossed arms.

Unsure as to whether he was making fun of her, she answered seriously, "Sometimes. I usually ride late in the day, because of the heat."

Suspecting that his smile had been misinterpreted, he assured her, in a complimentary way, "Oh, I think it's great! Most people I know would be afraid to go out in the dark on a lonely country road."

She smiled and said carelessly, "I might be afraid in town, I guess. But not out here. No one ever bothers you."

Alan offered to show her some paintings he was working on. The house he had rented was very old, probably built in the 1930s, but had been kept in fair condition. It was not much more than a bungalow, a compact place with one bedroom, a tiny bathroom, a narrow little kitchen, and one large, L-shaped room which served as the living and dining area. In this large room Alan had put all his paints and equipment and canvasses, in front of a picture window without curtains. There were no curtains or blinds on any of the windows. Suitcases and boxes were scattered here and there on the worn hardwood floor. Elaine recognized some pieces of furniture which had been in the house before: a threadbare sofa, a few wooden chairs, a white plastic coffee table, an old brass fire screen on the hearth, and some painted bookcases, on top of which now sat a small television topped by rabbit ear antenna and a portable stereo.

Alan joked about the place's obvious lack of luxury and showed Elaine some of his works in progress. They were much like the colorful paintings from the faculty art show. She lied and said that she liked them. After this she helped him unpack a few boxes. One small box was full of books, all of them about art, photography or music. She arranged them on the bookshelf for him.

But Elaine was careful not to outstay her welcome. She soon made her excuses.

"Are you sure you can get home all right?" he asked, stepping out the front door with her. "I'm not sure I feel right about you riding home in the dark."

"Oh, there's no problem," she said, happy for his concern. "I've done it before. Besides, there's a full moon out."

He looked up at the sky. The moon, a pure cool white now, was just clearing the tops of the pine forest that surrounded the house and yard.

"Well, all right," he consented. "As long as there aren't any werewolves in these parts."

She laughed. Alan thanked her for her help, and as she mounted her horse he casually remarked, "Come and see me now and then. It's going to be a little lonely here."

"I will," she said, catching her breath.

On the ride home she let the reins go slack and didn't bother much with the horse. The animal knew the way home and walked at a brisk pace.

She was thinking of Alan—his face, his smile, and every word he had spoken to her that evening. He had invited her to visit him! Wasn't this a privilege he was denying other friends? He seemed to feel comfortable with her, so much so that her presence was not considered an intrusion. Yes, he liked her, and Elaine felt that if she could hide her deeper feelings, nothing would change that. At least she would have him for a friend.

Her horse passed by a swampy area where the continual, vibrant croaking of tree frogs filled the air. The sound roused Elaine from her preoccupation, and she was surprised to see how far they had come already. Ahead she could see the street light that glowed over the intersection of the highway and Harrison Road. She looked behind her as a car approached, and saw two elongated silhouettes of horse and rider, a forked shadow from the light of the street lamp, and the moon.

Elaine decided to wait at least three or four days before she took up Alan's invitation. She wouldn't let herself hope that his feelings for her would change—at least not consciously—yet she was happy, and rode the rest of the way home that night feeling very grateful for the bit of good fortune which had come her way at last.

*   *   *   *   *   *

That night, she found it difficult to sleep. She kept seeing Alan's face, and hearing his invitation to come and visit, her thoughts branching off into multitudes of fantasies. Close to two in the morning, she finally fell asleep, but was shortly awakened by a terrific thunderstorm.

Through the closed blinds, the constant lightning at first looked like the changing illumination of a great fire. The thunder was booming, and sometimes made the furniture in her room vibrate. Elaine saw the night light in her bathroom go out momentarily. She went to the window and opened the blinds. Strong winds were tossing the trees about. She had seldom seen lightning so continuous and dazzling. It was sheet lightning, and lit up the clouds in different parts of the sky simultaneously. Every few seconds the heavens were as bright as a dawn sky. She wondered how Alan was faring in his little house in the midst of this storm, and imagined him at his window, watching the same spectacular light show.

Elaine tried to sleep again, but gave up after an hour or so of tossing and turning. Feeling a little hungry, she got up and walked down the hall toward the kitchen, but before she reached the den, a strange noise stopped her in her tracks. A loud crackling, buzzing sound had startled her. It sounded something like the hum of a powerful electric line. She peeked around the doorway, and a dim light from the kitchen revealed an open window, through which several large insects had entered the house. She saw several moths, a beetle, and the source of the strange noise in her ears, a large brown dragonfly which kept buzzing around and tapping itself against the ceiling. Elaine quickly closed the window and the doors to the den, leaving the insects for her father to deal with in the morning, and took an alternate route to the kitchen, where she made herself some chocolate chip cookies.

Chapter Six

Elaine saw Alan again sooner than she had planned. Two days after their chance meeting at his house, as she was riding along the main road, a car slowed beside her. Alan leaned out the window and waved something in his hand.

"I finally got around to developing those pictures," he said. "One's of you. Want to see them?"

When his car was out of sight Elaine prodded her horse into a run, and slowed down to a walk again when she was about a quarter of a mile from his house. Alan was taking a small box out of the trunk of his car as she rode inside the gate. He put the box on the front steps and walked over to her as she dismounted.

"She's beautiful. A palomino?" he asked.

"Yes."

He stroked the animal's sinewy neck as Elaine hitched her to a rusty clothes line post.

"What's her name?"

"Cherry. The first owner called her that, so I just kept the name."

"She's a lovely color."

As they walked into the house Elaine noticed that Alan was glancing at her hair.

"I wasn't sure the other night—have you done something to your hair?" he asked curiously.

"It always gets a little blonde if I'm out in the sun a lot in the summer."

"Looks nice," he said, and immediately picked up a folder from a chair and began showing her the photographs he had taken.

This was the first time he had ever complimented her on her appearance. As he flipped through the pictures he stood very near, his arm touching hers, their faces close together. She was much more conscious of his nearness than the photographs before her eyes.

"A few turned out better than I expected," Alan remarked.

She said that she liked all of them, but groaned when he came to the picture of her he had taken on campus.

"Here you are in your brunette days."

"Oh, I look terrible!"

"No, you don't!" he protested laughingly, nudging her arm. "What do you mean? It's a good picture. I think I'll frame it."

"Please don't."

"I was only kidding. But I do like it. I'll make you a copy if you want one."

"No, thanks!"

He smiled at her emphatic answer and shook his head. They went into the kitchen to get something cold to drink. She saw that the refrigerator was full of food now, noticing bottles of juice, and packages with labels she had seen in a health food store.

"A friend who said I was eating too much junk got me started on this stuff," Alan muttered, surveying the contents of the refrigerator with a hesitant expression. "But I don't think it'll do me any good until I stop smoking."

He poured out some "natural" apple juice. Elaine sipped the muddy-looking liquid and pretended to enjoy it.

Everything in the house was much as she had left it; there was no sign that any work had been done—no painting, nor any further unpacking. A stereo radio was playing softly, and a paperback book was open on the sofa, where Alan plopped down to finish his drink. Elaine sat down opposite him on the raised brick hearth of the fireplace.

They talked about the house, and more of its idiosyncrasies he had discovered. After a while they somehow got on the subject of movies. It happened that they had both watched the same late show the night before, a screwball comedy of the thirties. They laughed again over favorite scenes, and brought up other films.

Elaine was in one of the lower heavens. It was intoxicating to have him all to herself, and with all the laughter and euphoria, she even got a little silly. Alan asked her jokingly if the apple juice had gone to her head.

He decided to have some more juice, and asked Elaine, "Can I get you some more?"

"Let me get them," she said.

She jumped to her feet, and at once began blacking out.

* * * * * *

After a few moments Elaine was vaguely aware of Alan's voice saying something. At first it was muffled and unintelligible, like a voice heard underwater. Then, she slowly became aware of his arm

45

underneath her, supporting her. He had managed to catch her before she hit the floor. She opened her eyes wide and gradually blinked away the dissipating darkness.

"Elaine, are you all right?" he was asking, looking very uneasy.

"I'm sorry," she murmured, blinking slowly.

He helped her sit down on the sofa and asked her if this had ever happened to her before.

"A few times...I think it's low blood pressure."

He wanted to know if she had seen a doctor about this problem. She hesitated, but Alan kept questioning her, and even asked if she was taking some kind of medication. So that he would not think something worse of her, she told him about the prescription drugs that she was using.

Alan seemed concerned. He said he had some friends who had taken "those damn things."

"They can have serious side effects—I guess you know that," he went on. "But side effects worse than low blood pressure."

And he started rattling off a list of minor and major horrors, a few of which she hadn't of heard before.

"I don't mean to frighten you, Elaine, but I think it's something you should consider. Did you doctor tell you about these things before he gave you the pills?"

"Well, he said there could be side effects. I had indigestion at first, but it went away, and—"

He interrupted to ask how long she had been taking the medications, and was surprised that it had been so long.

"Do they really help that much?" he asked.

"Not much, I suppose. They help me sleep."

"You'd probably be better off if you just drank a glass of wine before bed—that's what I do. Why did you start taking the medications?"

It took her a few moments to work up the courage to tell him.

"I was depressed."

"How depressed?"

She couldn't bring herself to tell him.

"Just...depressed," she shrugged.

"Most teenagers get depressed. I was a pretty morose adolescent myself for a while. It's something you usually grow out of. I don't think it's a good idea to stay on those drugs for extremely long periods of time."

All the while, he had been talking to her with a serious, steady look that held her eyes. He kept looking at her when he paused and waited for her to say something.

"I—suppose I should quit using them," she said, looking to him questioningly.

"I think that would be a good idea, Elaine," he said approvingly. "Talk to your doctor, and see if he thinks you're ready. You may not need them anymore."

When Elaine left his house later that day she rode straight home and called her therapist. He was very pleased that she was feeling well enough to get along without the drugs, and told her how to start reducing the dosages gradually. She started the process the next morning.

*　　*　　*　　*　　*　　*

Elaine soon convinced her parents that it was time for her to go off her medication. They were wary at first, but, wishing to believe that a horrific episode in their lives and that of their daughter was over and done with, they finally consented. She didn't tell them that she had already begun to cut down. She was already suffering a slight malaise, the physical effect of withdrawal. It grew much worse during the next few days, but she waited, and endured.

One night was particularly bad for her. The malaise was intense, almost unbearable. She was weak and shaky, and couldn't fall asleep. She stayed in bed the following day, but gradually felt better. That night, after eating a little cereal, she went back to bed and slept soundly until morning. Even a booming thundershower didn't wake her.

Elaine slept late. When she woke up the sunlight was pouring in obliquely through an east-facing window. Though still somewhat weak and unwell, she felt wonderfully fit compared to the day before, and for a while at least, relieved of that torment, she also felt as though she had been changed somehow, made new, like the bright shafts of morning sun that were streaming into her room.

She got out of bed and went to the window, where a beautiful and unexpected sight met her eyes. Outside the glass, a spider had spun a web which, secured at each corner of the window, covered it entirely in an airy, intricate tracery. The web might have been invisible except for innumerable tiny beads of water hanging from every filament at almost regular intervals, and each one transformed into a diamond by the sun.

For some reason, Elaine took it as a good omen.

The worst of her ordeal seemed to be over, so she decided to go and see Alan. As she rode out of her yard, the fragrance of mimosa blooms filled her nostrils. She breathed in its sweetness, feeling some little pleasure in things again for the first time in many days.

*   *   *   *   *   *

Alan seemed relieved to see Elaine again after nearly a week and a half.

"I was going to get to a phone today and call you," he said.

He had experienced some misgivings about giving medical advice to her, and had become a little worried about her absence. She looked drawn and somewhat pale, but otherwise seemed fine. Alan asked her if she had okayed everything with her doctor and her parents. Elaine assured him that she had done all this, and that getting off the drugs was what she wanted. She exaggerated the ease with which she was ending her dependency on the medications, and even told him that she was feeling better without them.

He didn't know that he was the only reason she had stopped using the drugs — that he was the single source of hope and joy that made them unnecessary for her now.

She began to visit Alan more often, and he never seemed to mind that she appeared at his house so frequently. If there had been any resentment on his part she knew that she would have sensed it, but usually he seemed glad to see her, or else accepted her presence there as a friend's right. Sometimes Elaine feared that the frequency of her visits would make him suspicious that she had feelings for him. The thought that he might know she loved him was dreadful to her, and yet she longed to tell him.

Alan had always impressed her as very even-tempered person. He never seemed to lose a certain basic composure and self-possession. She had seldom seen him angry, disturbed or sad. Yet since the recommencement of their friendship it became apparent to her that he was preoccupied about something, and quite restless. Often when she came over she would find him working in the yard, or making pleasant but unnecessary improvements and repairs to the house—just to stay busy, it seemed to her.

As far as she could tell Alan was not doing much painting. He told her he had been doing some photography, but she saw little evidence of it. Elaine wondered about his air of preoccupation and restlessness; it worried her a little. She wanted him to be content. Yet, at the same time, she could not help wishing that things would continue just as they were, since it meant that he had more time for her.

Before long Alan began to include her in his restless diversions. One day, out of the blue, he suggested that they go into town for a movie.

Elaine tried not to show too much eagerness when she agreed to come along. She had never been in his car before. Sitting by his side, she relished the feeling of being a couple with him. At the theater, she was filled with pride and delight when she saw that they were being observed by some college students who knew them both. After the film they drove to an oriental restaurant, bought some food and took it back to his house.

The next day Elaine purchased a cookbook and began experimenting with several Asian dishes at home. She discovered that she had a natural talent for cooking, and when she felt confident enough of this new cuisine, she prepared a dinner at Alan's house. He took a few bites and asked her if she wanted a job as his private chef. After this success she prepared a meal for him at least twice a week.

They began to go out together fairly often—to restaurants, to stores, movies, and concerts in the park. Once he even suggested that they drive to Atlanta for the day, but then changed his mind about it. They went instead to some famous gardens near Columbus. As they strolled through the greenhouses and the outdoor sections, Alan took lots of photographs.

The pictures from the gardens inspired him. Suddenly he was flooded with ideas, and began painting for hours each day. This was in late July. Careful not to make a nuisance of herself while he was feeling creative, Elaine came over less frequently during the week, but was always there, and always welcome, on the hot, lazy summer weekends. In the evenings they would sit out on the screened back porch, with cold drinks in hand, in the breeze of a noisy old oscillating fan Alan had found in the attic. They looked out on the backyard, where there was a level area surrounded by a small ornamental wire fence. It had once been a garden, but was now full of tall grasses, and morning glory vines that twined around rotting stakes and the rusty wire fence. Alan said he wished he had moved in during the spring, so that he could have planted a vegetable garden there. He thought he might clear off a spot and plant some cool weather vegetables toward the end of the summer. Elaine volunteered to help.

She talked with her friend Marion on the phone several times a week, but they saw each other infrequently, since she had a new job and a new boyfriend. She knew about Alan Reese living nearby, and Elaine's feelings for him. Fearing that an emotional disaster was in store for her friend, Marion tried to gently dissuade her from putting much hope in this relationship, but Elaine thought Marion had too poor a track record with the opposite sex to give sound advice.

Elaine's parents were unaware that Alan Reese was renting a house in the neighborhood. They thought Elaine was out riding all the while she was with him, or with Marion. They seldom questioned her, as she gave them little cause for concern nowadays. They were relieved that she seemed to be in better spirits, and taking an interest in things again.

One weekend in late August Alan went out of town to see his sister in Atlanta. When he came back he found that the unsightly area in the backyard had been cleared, and that a little garden had been planted there. Elaine had filled it with flowers she had dug from the overflow of her mother's garden at home. They were chrysanthemums and coreopsis, all in bloom.

Chapter Seven

One Sunday they spent a few hours at a country arts and crafts fair which was held every year in a little town near Columbus. Around noon, while Elaine and Alan were looking for a certain concession they had noticed earlier, a display of handmade jewelry in one of the rustic booths caught her eye. They stopped there briefly.

Elaine particularly liked an old fashioned-looking filigree pendant of vermeil. It was not very expensive, and she considered buying the piece, but after a few moments she placed it back on the display case with a regretful smile.

"Why don't you get it?" Alan asked her.

"Oh, I don't need it," she said.

The truth was that she didn't have the cash to spare at present, even for this small luxury. She had spent most of her money for the month the previous weekend, and was being frugal with what she had left. Alan noticed the way she fingered her purse as she gazed at the pendant wistfully.

After leaving the jewelry booth, they soon found the food concession they had been looking for. They bought some lunch and dined under the colorful canopy of a small pavilion. As soon as Alan finished his meal he excused himself, and was gone for a few minutes. When he came back Elaine was waiting for him outside the tent.

Later on, while they were standing in a crowd of people listening to fiddle players, Alan drew something out of his pocket, and, with a cryptic smile, took Elaine's hand and placed the filigree pendant in her upturned palm.

"I want you to have that," he said, his smile no longer mysterious but affectionate.

She was dumbfounded at first as she stared down at her hand. She raised her eyes to his with a moved, questioning look, but immediately lowered them again so that he wouldn't see that look. She admired the gift and thanked him for it with the proper degree of friendly appreciation, all the while wanting to run off somewhere and weep. But that had to wait until she was alone in her room later that day.

This gift, and other gestures of affection and friendship, made Elaine wonder what she really meant to him. Earlier she had seen no evidence that he loved her in the way she loved him, and somewhere deep inside she knew that he probably never would. Yet recent circumstances had strengthened a feeble hope in her that would not die. Did his gestures of affection, and his exclusive companionship, mean that his feelings for her might be changing? The signs were confusing. Alan was always kind to her, and on rare and precious occasions, something a little more—yet he had always kept a certain distance. She knew all about his likes and dislikes in everything from food to literature, and about his background and experiences, but anything more deeply personal was seldom confided in her. There were no delvings into past loves, or present secret troubles, or innermost longings for the future, and no matter how much she revealed about her problems, her inner life, he was almost always reserved about his own. Elaine saw that as yet there were definite boundaries to their friendship, that she could approach only so far. But wasn't there at least a possibility that this could change in time, and that he might someday begin to confide in her?

She was changing, after all. She had begun to accomplish things which gave her a little pride—her photography and cooking, for example—small achievements that were important events in her life, since they indicated that the dire, relentless voice within her, the one that constantly told her that she would not fail to fail, was a liar. Before, she had always been afraid of trying new things for fear of failure, but Alan's friendship somehow gave her courage, and she gained more confidence in her own abilities.

Elaine even thought herself prettier these days. She was slimmer, her complexion had cleared, and she had stopped using most of the heavy make-up she had worn since high school, having detected Alan's dislike for it. At times, she sensed that he was attracted to her, but didn't know for certain, and she still kept wondering if his feelings for her had changed at all.

*   *   *   *   *   *

From the first, Alan considered Elaine an exceptionally bright and well-read girl, but even before he learned about her problem with depression, he noticed her sadness and isolation, and suspected that she was a troubled young woman. He felt somewhat sorry for her, and at school was especially friendly and attentive with her. He befriended her out of compassion at first, but then came to genuinely like her. When they met again during the summer he was pleased to see her, although this time his friendship was mixed with self-interest, since he had quickly discovered that he didn't much like his self-imposed solitude, and knew that he would be glad for some company now and then.

He wanted to help Elaine with her emotional problems, and thought the best way of doing this was to simply offer his friendship, along with a little advice at times, in the form of some books on psychology and oriental philosophy that he lent her to read.

According to his own philosophy of inner well-being, unhappiness was a sign of unhealthiness and weakness. He was unhappy only when he allowed himself to indulge in unreasonable or unattainable desires, and consequently always strove to avoid or suppress such desires. He had always been successful enough— except in the past year or so. Recently, his frustration over an inability to control himself, along with certain circumstances, had been doing some damage to his ego, and Elaine's infatuation with him had acted as a kind of balm to his ailing self-esteem.

Alan had suspected her infatuation while she was his student at the college. He became sure of it on the last day of class, and didn't know how to respond except with an obvious coldness toward her. During the summer, in a more informal, isolated setting, he still kept his emotional distance, but for selfish reasons saw her more than he should have. Telling himself that his friendship was good for her, he encouraged her to feel free to visit whenever she wished.

Towards the end of the summer, Alan realized that he was attracted to her, but gave no serious consideration to an intimacy of that sort. He considered Elaine unusually immature and naïve in some ways, but worst of all, beneath her unvarying politeness and ladylike restraint, he perceived a frighteningly lean and hungry look. And then there was her depression and emotional fragility. All this kept him from indulging in any casual relationship with her.

Besides, he was in love with someone else.

*   *   *   *   *   *

One afternoon in late August Elaine went to Alan's house to take him some bread she had baked herself. She drove over in her car, under a dark, thickly clouded sky which was threatening to rain at any moment. By the time she reached his driveway it had begun to pour. Alan held the front door open as she ran up the steps with her package. He caught the smell of freshly baked bread and followed her into the kitchen. She told him that she wasn't going to stay, but he replied, "Why not?" and invited her to have supper with him, since she had supplied the best part of it.

After the meal they went out to sit on the back porch and watch the rain, which was coming down so hard and heavy that there were already big pools of water on the lawn. Elaine worried about the flowers she had planted, and had visions of them washing away.

"Don't worry, they'll survive," said Alan carelessly, taking a sip from his glass of wine.

Soft, fitful breezes brought them the sweet smell of the jasmine flowers blooming on a spindly trellis by the screen door. Alan asked her if she had been writing lately. Once she had timidly shown him a short story she had written, a science fiction tale about the end of the world. He thought that the story was very bleak, but liked her writing, and encouraged her to keep with it.

She told him that she had just finished another story and a poem.

"They're not about the end of the world, are they?" he asked with a faint smile.

Elaine smiled and nodded.

"They just come out that way," she said, shrugging.

At nightfall, Alan was restless. He found a newspaper he had purchased that morning, and they perused the movie listings for the theaters in town. Nothing interested him, but Elaine noticed that *Great Expectations* was scheduled for that evening on television.

"That's a great film," she remarked.

"Is it? Well, you're the movie expert. Why don't you stay and watch it with me?"

Alan moved the television set from the bookcase to the plastic table in front of the sofa. The sofa was rather small, so he and Elaine were quite close to one another when they sat down together.

The movie began. It hadn't been on long when Alan got up, went into the kitchen, and came back with a full glass of wine. He paused behind the sofa.

"Sorry, I forgot to offer you some wine—would you care for some?"

"No, thanks."

Before he sat down again he switched off the overhead light, so that the only illumination in the room was that from the television, and a dim glow from a fluorescent lamp in the kitchen. Alan sat down heavily, spilling a few drops of wine on her.

"Sorry."

"That's all right," said Elaine, wiping off the drops of liquid from her bare arm.

He was sitting even closer to her now, and of this she was keenly conscious, but she kept her eyes on the television screen.

Alan seemed unusually quiet as they sat together, and she had the feeling that his mind was not on the movie, fine as it was. About a quarter of an hour passed, and it was sometime after that when Elaine became aware that he was watching her. She felt his eyes on her, and abruptly her heart began to pound, slowly at first. Finally, when she turned her face to him, his eyes weren't on her; he was taking the last sip of his wine. The next moment he leaned forward and sat the empty glass on the table.

As he sat back against the sofa he put his feet up on the table and stretched out to a more comfortable position. He was so close to Elaine that his arm was pressed against hers. She wondered if he could feel how her heart was beating.

They both sat unmoving for a while, and though her eyes were fixed on the television screen and following the movements of faces and figures there, she was aware of only him.

Elaine felt him nestle closer to her, and turn his face toward her. With a pounding heart she turned to him. His eyes were closed. He was asleep! She felt like a fool.

Alan sighed and sank down a little more, resting his head on her shoulder. Despite her mortification, his nearness filled her with bittersweet emotion. She leaned closer and gave him the lightest kiss on his forehead, but the next instant, as she gazed at that placid face, she felt a resentment welling up in her for the first time.

Elaine looked away from him and stared at the television, frowning, and suppressing the tears that came into her eyes. Only one fell.

About an hour later, as Alan woke and opened his eyes, he looked up at Elaine. Mellow with wine, he studied the pleasant lines of the face so close to his own. He made the slightest movement closer to her, in a warm, amorous, drowsy state, but suddenly caught himself, waking fully. He quickly sat up, took a deep breath, and stretched out his arms and legs with exaggerated movements.

"Sorry," he said somewhat nervously. "I fell asleep. Too much wine, I guess."

Pretending to be absorbed in the film, and unaware that he had been awake before that moment, Elaine gave him only a brief, unsmiling glance. As the movie drew to a close, Alan reflected on how he had just come close to a minor disaster, exhaling several sighs of relief.

When the film was over, Elaine drove herself home in the slackening rain.

Chapter Eight

Elaine had realized the foolishness and hopelessness of her feelings for Alan, and that realization stayed with her depressingly, and didn't fade. Five days passed before she returned to his house. She found him packing some small boxes into a crate.

"What are you doing?" she asked.

Alan looked up and saw her at the screen door.

"I thought I heard someone drive up," he said. "Come on in. I was just looking for some negatives I packed away in here."

"Have you found them?" She stood over him now, watching him with a doubtful, uneasy look.

"Oh, they're in there," he replied carelessly, nodding toward a cardboard box set apart from the rest.

"Oh."

When he finished packing away the boxes he looked up at her with a quizzical smile.

"It's been a while," he remarked.

"We were out of town," she lied.

He invited her to join him for a lunch of leftover Chinese food. She heated the meal on the stove while he washed up. When his plate was set before him on the table he took a bite of the food and made a face.

"My palate has been suffering in your absence, you know," he said, trying to make her smile. She didn't smile.

"This food's not bad," she answered, not looking up.

After lunch she walked out to the back yard to check on her little garden. Alan followed her out. The flowers she had planted there were wilted; some were dead and brittle.

"Why didn't you water them?" she asked irritably, as she went to fetch a watering can.

"I really haven't paid any attention to the yard lately. I thought the flowers would be all right for a while after that rain we had last week," he said, somewhat surprised by her tone.

"That was last week," she muttered.

Alan went back into the house as she watered the garden. After a few minutes she came to the screen door again to tell him that she was leaving.

"So soon?" he asked.

"I have to go somewhere with my parents," she said, lying again. She was moody, and felt as though she might cry at any moment, so she wanted to get away from him.

Alan walked her to her car.

"I'm sorry about the flowers," he apologized.

Elaine hung her head and shrugged.

"That's all right," she murmured.

"How about if I make it up to you by taking you out to dinner tomorrow night?" he suggested.

She looked up into his face a little wistfully.

"Let's go to that new place downtown," he went on, with a coaxing smile. "It's very expensive. We'll get dressed up, and I'll pick you up at your house."

Elaine's parents happened to be out of town for a few days, so she made no objections to this. He told her he would be there for her at seven.

*   *   *   *   *   *

It was approaching seven-thirty when Alan arrived the next evening. He apologized for his lateness, but offered no explanation.

The meal was delicious, and the evening very pleasant. Elaine was smiling again, at least a little, though she was constantly wondering about the meaning of this nice, somewhat lavish gesture, and about Alan's unusual mood. He had been very complimentary to her all evening, and oddly attentive. He smiled and laughed easily, at the slightest provocation, but at times, as though suddenly self-conscious about something, he would quickly change, and become more serious, earnest. Once or twice, she noticed an uneasy, preoccupied look about him.

They sat by a small stained glass window, at a secluded corner table. The lights in the restaurant were low. At their table two candles burned in frosted glass globes.

As they waited for dessert Alan drew a pack of cigarettes out of his coat pocket.

"Do you mind?" he asked.

She shook her head and took a sip of her tea. The waiter brought their desserts. Elaine finished her piece of chocolate cake before Alan even began to eat.

"That must be good," he remarked smilingly, putting out the

cigarette.

He turned his attention to his food, and Elaine watched him as he ate. For the greater part of a week, she had been suffering with the hopelessness of her situation. She even tried to convince herself that she hated him, or at least that she didn't care for him so much. But tonight, all her feelings and longings returned in a flood. A warning immediately sounded inside her.

Don't let him see. It might drive him away.

Yet as never before she wanted to tell him how she felt about him — and almost did.

Alan left his dessert half-finished.

"Too rich for me," he said, pushing away the plate.

When they pulled up to her house in his car, he surprised her by parking and turning off the engine. He said nothing at first. Finally Elaine asked him if he would like to come in for a while.

"No, I won't stay. I...just wanted to talk to you about something," he said uncomfortably.

"About what?"

"I just wanted to let you know..."

He paused, and she waited for the rest with a sinking feeling.

"I'll be going back to Atlanta next week. I won't be living here anymore."

"When did you decide this?" she asked, with no reaction except a frown.

"Very recently."

He cleared his throat and went on, "An old friend of mine is writing a book on the rural south. He wants me to do the photography for it. He got in touch with me about a week ago, and I've been thinking it over since then."

Looking straight ahead, Elaine acknowledged his words with a slow, almost imperceptible nod of her head.

"A book…"

"Yes."

She had the presence of mind to offer some congratulatory remarks, and he told her some details about the project with restrained enthusiasm.

"A couple of years ago I did some work in one of the areas Jack mentioned, and quite a few of the pictures I took then are my favorites. The next time you're over I'll show them to you."

Then with that sudden self-consciousness she had seen earlier he stopped, and said nothing more for a while.

Elaine was casting uncomfortable glances in every direction but his. Finally he broke the silence.

"I hope you won't be making yourself scarce in the next few days, like you did last week."

"No, I won't," she replied — an automatic politeness.

"We'll have to do this again before I leave," he said, attempting a cheerful tone.

"Yes," she agreed. "I enjoyed it."

"I'm glad you did."

He smiled and relaxed visibly, as though relieved to have gotten something unpleasant over with. A few moments later they said goodnight.

She heard his car rumbling slowly down the long gravel driveway as she locked the door behind her. She walked through a dark house to her room. She undressed and went to bed. But within a few minutes she was up again. She put on jeans and a t-shirt, left the house, and drove to his.

Alan was reading in bed when he heard the car outside. By the time he had thrown on some clothes and started out of the room she was at the door, about to knock, but saw him through the screen and lowered her hand.

"Elaine!" he said, peering at her strangely as he came to the door.

Her expression was solemn and apprehensive.

"Is something wrong?" he asked.

"No."

He unlatched the door and opened it for her.

She stepped in, but stopped just inside the door, and she leaned against the door frame as she hung her head and tried to speak. Alan stood opposite her in an open shirt, his head lowered like hers, with a carefully neutral expression. His arms were folded across his chest, his shoulders raised awkwardly the least bit. He knew why she was here.

"What is it?" he asked gently.

Elaine closed her eyes for a moment, and took a long, deep breath before she answered.

"I love you," she murmured, unable to look into his eyes.

Alan said nothing.

"I want to be with you," she said.

Another silence.

"That wouldn't be a good idea, Elaine," he answered.

"Why not?" she asked sadly, fearing what he would say next.

"More than one reason…but I think it's enough to say that I don't—I don't love you—not in that way."

She still could not bring herself to look at him, but managed to say, "I thought that might change."

"It won't."

She nodded quickly at this, to stop him from repeating such a painful answer, or adding any more to it.

"I'm sorry this happened," he said.

She glanced up at him for an instant to see his expression.

"You knew, didn't you?" she asked, in a hurt tone.

He hesitated.

"I guess I suspected — recently —"

"Then why — ?" she began, with a pained, angry expression that immediately faded, though some anger remained in her voice as she said, "You must have just felt sorry for me."

"I care about you, Elaine."

She winced as though receiving a physical blow.

"I'm sorry," she said. "I don't have any right to be angry with you. It's not your fault."

She was looking at him now. Her hand was finding the handle of the screen door.

"I'll leave you alone now. I'm sorry I bothered you."

"It's all right, Elaine."

She opened the door.

"I don't want you to feel bad about all this," he said.

She walked down the steps wondering just how that was possible.

* * * * * *

Elaine didn't even try to sleep that night. Alone in the house, she turned on the television and plopped down in her father's recliner in front of it. Throughout the long hours, she got up only once, to take aspirin for a headache. At daylight she made coffee and tried to read the newspaper.

During the day she was able, for a while at least, to keep out of her thoughts the constant, painful repetition of what had happened the night before. All night, the scene had repeated itself in her mind over and over again, and each time the same thought came afterwards. If only she hadn't gone over to Alan's house and said those things—at least she could have spared herself the pain and humiliation of it. Why, why had she gone there? To find out what she already knew! And what in the world had possessed her to think that he could love her! It seemed incredible to her now that she had gone to him with any such hope. It struck her as so fantastical now that the memory of it was like a bad dream. She was amazed at herself, and was tortured by the thought of how odd and laughable it all must have seemed to him.

She wished she had never met him. She wished she were dead.

Elaine had promised her parents that she would keep the house clean while they were gone. She wanted something to occupy her mind and hands, so she turned on her stereo and listened to the loud music for several hours while she dusted, vacuumed, scrubbed, washed and dried clothes and linens, and emptied trashcans. In the afternoon, took a portable radio with earphones outside and pulled weeds, cleaned out the stable, and mowed the lawn.

After such exertions in the heat, she felt a headache coming on. Exhausted, she sat down in the shade to cool off a little before going into the air-conditioned house. Elaine watched a mockingbird which had been waiting in the trees flit down to the grass to get the insects which had been killed, mangled, or brought out by the mower. An unfortunate grasshopper with only one leg hobbled into the shady part of the yard from the open lawn, slowly making its way through a patch of ivory and lemon yellow toadstools near her.

"Sorry, bug," she murmured, regretful for what had happened to the grasshopper, but somberly likening herself to this helpless, wounded, doomed creature.

Having heard the postman's vehicle earlier in the day, she walked down the driveway to fetch the mail. There was only one item in the box, a letter from Ned. She read it as she walked back to the house, not really absorbing much of its specifics, but noting its cheery, playful tone. At least someone in the world was happy, she reflected, while feeling sorry for herself again.

Later Elaine prepared a light supper, made some brownies, and, after a shower, sat down in front of the television set, filling her stomach with chocolate and milk until midnight. At last, drowsy and exhausted, she fell into her bed and fell asleep within a few minutes.

But less than three hours later, she woke up. She immediately tried to sleep again, but only tossed and turned, as she fought against the painful memories of her last conversation with Alan, weeping as she thought of how foolish and adoring she had been, and how he would never love her—for that matter, how no one would ever love her. She couldn't control the irrational thoughts which presented themselves over and over again, desperate and tumultuous.

Finally, toward the early morning hours, Elaine fell into a light sleep, but it was a troubled slumber, like a door closing on a scene of riot, chaos, and noise in the next room, only muffled and temporarily out of sight. And waking was the instant, overwhelming resumption of that scene in the next room, spilling out through the door as it opened, and consuming.

Weary and muddled, Elaine rose early. She made strong coffee to clear her head, dressed herself, went outside and ran down the driveway and the road until she could feel her heart pounding and the blood pumping through her veins. Stretching her limbs, she gazed up at the masses of white and gray in the northwestern sky, an alpine scene of bright clouds which, heaped one upon the other, resembled the snow-capped peaks of a mountain range reflecting the morning light. As she walked back home she was calmer, and though the obsessive, nearly ungovernable thoughts and images still preyed on her mind, they gradually diminished, becoming vaguer and fainter each time, like the rumblings of a departing storm. After breakfast Elaine turned on the television again to occupy her thoughts.

It was a relief when, just before noon, her parents arrived back home unexpectedly early. Their company and conversation were at least a helpful distraction. They were pleasantly surprised with all the household chores and yard work their daughter had done, and rewarded her generously with cash.

In the late afternoon Elaine answered the ringing telephone. Alan was calling from somewhere in town.

"I meant to call you earlier," he said, "but I had some car trouble, and couldn't get to a phone till just now. I would have stopped by, but I didn't know if you would want me to."

Elaine made no answer.

"I just wanted to know," he went on, "if you were all right...I was a little worried about you."

"I'm all right," she said.

"That's good."

After another silence he said, "Well, I just wanted to check on you. I'll let you go now. I'll see you later."

She went riding, was out for hours, and that night finally slept out of sheer physical exhaustion.

The following morning her mother was planning to have some guests to the house. To avoid them Elaine decided to go horseback riding again and left early. Dressed in a new white blouse, tan jodhpurs and a hard black riding cap she sometimes wore, she rode north for a few miles along the main road to some pastureland. She stopped at a creek and sat in the shade of the willows there—but only for a little while. Painful memories and thoughts came to her, and as soon as her horse finished a leisurely drink at the water she remounted and rode away, as though hoping to leave those thoughts behind her in that place. She left the pasture and started back down the highway.

Eventually she came to road which led to Alan's house. She had avoided it the day before, but this time she turned down it instead of passing on, though she wasn't sure that she could bring herself to see him again, or even that she wanted to. There seemed to be little purpose in it.

As Elaine neared his place she caught a glimpse of his car through the hedge. Out of habit her horse slowed her pace near the driveway; Cherry was about to turn in there, but Elaine suddenly made her go on past, prodding her with a kick. Passing by the open gate, she looked in and saw a second car parked in the yard. She stopped, turned around, and rode back to the gate, but paused there for only an instant, because she had seen Alan coming out of the house with a young woman.

Elaine quickened her horse to a canter. It was only when she reached the highway that she slowed down to a walk again. A car passed her—the one she had seen at Alan's house, and in it a young woman was driving alone. Elaine watched her until she was out of sight. She was close to home when she heard another automobile approaching, and she turned and saw Alan's car. He slowed down, gestured to her, and then pulled ahead of her and parked on the side of the road. Elaine walked her horse slowly to the driver's side of the car. He turned off the engine and looked up at her.

"Hey," he said. "I saw you riding by the house."

Cherry decided that she didn't like being so close to a car, and started forward slightly. Elaine made the mare step back, and, looking down at Alan she waited, saying nothing.

"I intended to come and see you yesterday," he said, shading his eyes against the brilliant late morning sun behind her. "I wanted to explain something to you."

"About that woman?" she asked. There was no emotion in her voice, and her eyes had a look of weariness, deathliness.

"Her name is Carol. Her arrival here today was totally unexpected. I didn't think we would ever get together again—we had decided before that it was all over..."

Alan stopped, wondering momentarily why he felt that he had to tell her these things. Elaine sat motionless as a statue. Alan had expected a more emotional reaction, and was somewhat relieved that she appeared so calm. She looked down on him with what seemed to be a sober dignity, an appearance enhanced, perhaps, by her formal riding clothes and erect posture in the saddle. But Elaine felt anything but dignified at that moment.

"I'm leaving kind of early tomorrow," he continued. "I wanted to see you before I left, and tell you that I care about you very much. I'm going to write to you. I'll send you my address."

"I wish you wouldn't," she replied.

Alan hesitated, but responded, "Maybe you're right...but I'll send you my address, and you can write back to me if you change your mind."

There was a trace of hardness and impatience in his voice now which hurt her, but she remained impassive.

"Well," he sighed, looking at a loss. "I wish we could part as friends."

"We do."

He squinted against the blinding sun that shone out all around her face and flashed above the peak of her cap, trying to discover if her expression belied the answer she had given so readily.

"Are you sure?" he asked doubtfully.

"Of course. I wish you luck with your book."

"Thank you, Elaine."

He added gently, "You're so talented...I wish you'd give yourself a chance. Did you know you're very pretty?"

And he smiled at her in a way that tore at her heart, because she saw condescension and pity mixed in with unmistakable affection. Unable to answer, she looked off straight ahead. Finally she told him that she had to be getting home.

"Will I see you again before I leave?" he asked her.

"I think I'd like to say goodbye now."

"If that's how you want it."

"Yes."

So after a brief exchange of meaningless pleasantries, they parted, each going away from the other with a feeling of relief.

*   *   *   *   *   *

It was time to register again for the fall term at the college. Elaine had no desire to return to school, but there seemed nothing else for her to do. If she stayed at home to wallow in her misery, her parents would surely send her back to the hospital. Leaving home was no option, either; she had no money to live on her own, and the thought of going out into the world and perhaps getting a job terrified her. She wished that some debilitating illness would strike her, or better yet, a fatal one.

Cowardly when it came to physical pain, she tried to think of quick and easy ways to die. The best, surest method, she thought, must be a bullet to the head. But she had no gun, and didn't even know anyone who did. She was hesitant to attempt to purchase one, for fear that someone might become suspicious and alert her parents. Her parents had long since sold the cabin on the river, so there was no gas stove to try again. Then one day Elaine read a newspaper article about a local man who had committed suicide by sitting in his car in a closed garage. This seemed like a painless, easy death, and she could do it when her parents went away on vacation. She decided that, if no better way presented itself, that this method would be her default. It would be the perfect way to go, she thought, provided that she could have the house to herself long enough to fill the garage with enough carbon monoxide to do the job. For some reason, her parents' visit to Savannah and Charleston had been postponed, but she knew that they would eventually take a trip and leave her alone at the house for a week or so.

It was a kind of comfort to have this plan of escape in place, however vague it remained. It was at least a deadline to suffering—suffering to which, otherwise, she saw no end. In the meantime, Elaine decided to deaden her pain somewhat by going back on the antidepressants and tranquilizers Her mother and father were disappointed when she resumed her medications, but a little encouraged that she went back to school in September and did well in her courses.

On campus Elaine kept her usual low profile and lunched with her father often. At home she went riding nearly every day the weather would permit. As usual she went out into the fields and woods, sat by creeks and watched the tumbling waters, and at night, went up to the roof to stargaze.

In late October Elaine's mother had to undergo a hysterectomy. She recovered slowly, and was home every day for nearly an entire month. The autumn weather was mild, but December turned bitterly cold, and a freakish snow storm occurred just before Christmas.

Elaine had never seen her yard and the countryside covered in a white blanket. She put on her brother's work boots and traipsed about in the snow, exploring the effects of this extraordinary phenomenon. In the sunlight the limbs of trees glittered with icicles, and when a breeze blew, they made a crackling sound and sent little showers of ice to the ground. Hardly anyone could drive on the roads, and college classes were canceled for the entire week. The electricity was out for two days, and a kindly neighbor dropped off a supply of firewood on his tractor. Elaine's mother, still convalescing somewhat from her operation, spent this time on the couch in the den in front of the fire, and at night, they played cards and read by candlelight.

*   *   *   *   *   *

In the coldest weeks of the winter, Elaine spent a lot of time in her room going through old papers and mementos. Sitting on the floor, she opened the large bottom drawer of her dresser, where she kept a bunch of photographs, keepsakes, letters and notebooks. The drawer was less than half full now; once it had held so much that she could hardly close it. She had destroyed most of its contents when she was seventeen, just before her suicide attempt.

Elaine began to take out the papers and other things and place them in front of her on the floor. This was the first time she had gone through them in almost a year, and she began to experience a kind of deja vu. But another feeling was even stranger, and so strong that she paused a while, and looked down at the papers without really seeing them. She felt as though she were back in time somewhere many months past—as if the intervening months had never happened, or had passed in an instant like a dream. She was back there again, back where she had started, on an afternoon like this when she sat down to pick out and throw away things not meant for anyone's eyes but her own. Everything was much the same as it had been then, she realized. The sickly, familiar oppression she felt then she felt now, only it had come back with a vengeance She found some short stories and poems she had written this year and hidden at the bottom of the drawer and put them in a cardboard box.

Later, in the spring, she took the cardboard box outside and it to a place at the edge of the lawn, a spot near the paddock, where her father had burned some brush and small trees. It was an ugly, unkempt part of the lot. The grass was sparse, and the hard red earth showed everywhere around the big circle of charred wood and ashes. Pokeberry and nightshade had sprung up and fruited there.

Elaine placed the cardboard box atop the ashes, lit a match, and set fire to the papers.

When she walked into the house her mother was just hanging up the kitchen phone.

"Elaine, you just missed Ned. He wanted to speak to you. He was over at your Grandmother Adele's when I called her," said Mrs. Perdreau.

"I'm sorry I missed him."

"Well, you could come with us to Charleston next month, and

then you'd get to see him. We decided against going to Savannah right now, but after Charleston, we're driving up to the North Carolina mountains. You love the mountains, don't you?"

"I'll give Ned a call soon, or write to him."

"I know he'd love to see you. I wish you'd go with us."

"Uh, I'll think about it," Elaine answered, though she had no intention of going on a trip to North Carolina with her parents. For months she had been waiting for them to go away and leave her alone at the house.

Elaine walked to her room in a daze.

"One month, one month...," she was thinking as plopped down on her bed. "And Glen won't be home, either. One month, and they'll be gone. Then, I'll be gone."

Elaine was suddenly roused from her morbid thoughts by a knock at the bedroom door. Mrs. Perdreau looked in.

"I meant to tell you that Glen called earlier," she said. "He said he changed his mind about that trip with his friends, and he's coming home next month for the summer. Won't that be nice?"

Her mother closed the door, and it took a few moments for Elaine to fully comprehend what she had said—Glen was coming home. Her plans were ruined.

Chapter Nine

Elaine's eyes fluttered open, and the words from a poem in her dream fluttered out of her consciousness, instantly forgotten like the dream itself. She had been sleeping since they crossed the South Carolina state line, and a sudden jolt nearly rolled her onto the floorboard.

"Sorry, Elaine," said her father, who had hit the brakes to avoid another car carelessly turning into his lane.

She drew herself up in the seat and looked out on a familiar stretch of highway in Mount Pleasant. They had just passed the outskirts of the town, and the houses, sometimes in clusters, but few and far between, were mostly shabby and rustic. Farther on, a ramshackle produce stand preceded the last commercial center, which consisted of a laundromat, gas station, and a convenience store. After a few more houses and shanties, and a couple of wooden sheds where the basket ladies were closing down for the day, there was a long stretch of nothingness. Nothing but woods lined both sides of the highway, except for a few unpaved driveways marked by mailboxes.

The car slowed at one of these driveways and turned in. Woods of oak, wax myrtle, and palmettos were thick along the lengthy, winding dirt road. It branched off once into another private drive which led to the only other homestead on the Perdreau lands. Finally, the woods thinned out and gave way to an expansive yard, and Elaine could see her grandmother's place.

Mrs. Perdreau's home sat at the edge of a salt marsh, a large, two-story farmhouse of clapboard, with dark green shutters and a green metal roof. In the dusk, against the backdrop of a smoky red sunset, the old dwelling's white paint glowed with a reflected rosy light. A wide screened porch ran the entire length of the back of the house and wrapped around the side facing the marsh.

Elaine drank in the sight of a fondly remembered landscape where she had played as a child. Azalea bushes and small rose gardens were planted along the porch, and the grounds were dotted with magnolias, pines, cedars, palmettos and palms. But it was the great live oaks that she loved the most. Nearly a dozen of these beautiful old trees graced the yard. Their huge, tentacle-like limbs were draped with Spanish moss, and some of the lower branches were so massive and lengthy that they rested gnarled elbows on the ground. She looked for a tree house, which was still there in the largest of the oaks, and a rope swing, which was not. When her father parked the car in a graveled area near the house she could see more of the marsh, and the L-shaped dock she remembered well, its rough gray wooden posts exposed in the low tide.

The screen door opened, and Elaine's grandmother came down the steps smiling, followed by a young man.

"Oh, good," said Elaine's mother, "Ned's here, too."

Elaine turned and perked up a little at the mention of her cousin.

Seeing him, she made a conscious effort to put a smile on her face, or at least straighten out the usual frown.

Ned was a lanky teenager and not really that tall, but he looked big and brawny beside his slight, petite grandmother. He was wearing a red t-shirt, baggy khaki shorts, and muddy lace-up work boots over muddied socks that had probably once been white. His shirt bore the logo of a plant nursery where he was employed, and his skin was darkly tanned from working outside so much. A shank of light brown hair fell over one eyebrow. As the car came to a stop he ran up to it, cupped his hands around his face and pressed it up against Elaine's window with a goofy smile and googly eyes.

She smiled and shook her head. Same old Ned.

When she stepped out of the car he drew back with a melodramatic gesture and exaggerated surprise.

"Can it be?" he cried. "Is this little Elaine?"

His sudden bear hug made her squeak as she replied, "Hello, Ned."

Elaine's grandmother approached the car smiling, moist-eyed, with arms ready to embrace — first Mrs. Perdreau, who was first out of the car, then her son, and then Elaine. Ned helped with the luggage, but announced he had to get home to clean up and change his clothes.

"I promised some friends I would help 'em move, not realizing it was the day you folks would be here. Aren't I stupid?" he said, gazing at Elaine and awaiting a comeback to the opening he had given her. The two had always carried on a healthy trade in insults since early childhood.

"No argument here," she replied, but with poor comic timing, and more from old habit than a sense of humor, which had all but left her nowadays.

"Ow," he groaned, but then laughed, and gave her another hug before leaving.

She watched him shuffle down the driveway, his hands thrust down into the oversized pockets of his shorts. He walked a few hundred yards, but stopped at the bend of the driveway and turned his head, looking straight at Elaine, intensely, oddly for a moment, before his face broke into a broad smile. He gave a little wave and went on.

A frown returned to her face as she slowly followed her parents and her grandmother into the house. Ned isn't blind, she was thinking. He had already seen that something wasn't right with her.

The rooms of the house were filled with antiques, not many of them of great age or value, but all family heirlooms, some piece of which always elicited an envious sigh and compliments from Elaine's mother. They walked through the living room, an airy space with high ceilings and numerous windows which looked out on the marsh, and afterwards went into another room which was called the den, but looked like an old-fashioned parlor. Like the living room it had a high ceiling, but was smaller and cozier, and filled, almost crowded, with dark mahogany furniture: tables, bookcases, a curio cabinet, armchairs, a desk, and a big Chippendale style sofa. Everywhere there were antique or vintage vases and ornaments, and various picture frames with old black and white or hand-colored photographs of ancestors and other relatives. A huge, wine-colored Oriental rug, worn but still handsome, covered most of the hardwood floor. The three windows in the room had heavy curtains of dark crimson, and yellowish shades which filtered a mellow golden light on sunny days. On one wall was a stone fireplace with a flat, red brick hearth below and a thick wooden mantel shelf above covered with family pictures and knick-knacks.

Elaine lingered in this quiet and pleasant room after her parents and grandmother had gone on upstairs. Their voices died away, and all she could hear for a while was the ticking of the ornate mantel clock. She stretched out on the couch and closed her eyes, savoring the cool of the room, the dusky light, and the silence. There was something vaguely comforting here. Her grandmother's gentle presence was here in all her things — in the carefully dusted frames, the lace doilies on the faded upholstery, the quaint ceramic plaques with faded rose vines encircling a verse of scripture — even in the smell of the place, a faint mustiness which mingled with emanations from hidden sachets of potpourri, fragrant concoctions that she made herself from her flower gardens.

When Elaine finally left the room she went into the hall to follow the others upstairs, and at the foot of the steps nearly tripped over a little ball of gray fur which was suddenly between her feet. She then looked up and saw more kittens, black, white, and gray, pouncing down the steps after the first. On the landing the mother cat, a silver tabby, trotted past Elaine with wary looks.

She found her parents in one of the guest bedrooms, where her grandmother was checking the closet for sufficient linens.

"I'm sorry, dear," Elaine's mother was saying, "but I just can't share a room with cats."

"Oh, they're not supposed to be in here, and they know it. They're not even supposed to be in the house."

The elder Mrs. Perdreau emerged from the closet with a set of sheets and pillowcases.

"Where do I sleep, grandma?" asked Elaine.

"Do you remember that little bedroom off the den? You used to love it when you were little, and I thought you might want to use it again. If not, there's another guest room up here."

"I'll sleep downstairs," said Elaine, after a thoughtful pause. The first floor would give her more privacy, she realized, since all the other bedrooms were upstairs.

They went back down to the first floor, and Mrs. Perdreau seated her son and his family at the table in the breakfast room while she prepared supper, refusing any help. From where she sat Elaine had a view of the kitchen, and she watched her grandmother as she worked, thinking how much older she looked now. She was a small woman who, though frail-looking, enjoyed good health and energy for her eighty-one years. Her silvery gray hair was worn in a neat and changeless chignon. She was wearing one of her usual floral print house dresses, and comfortable dark leather shoes that looked a little bulky on her thin legs. Her voice was sometimes pleasant and steady, sometimes quavering and weak, and there was a slight trembling movement in her head and hands as she moved.

Mrs. Perdreau was a widow. Her husband, who had died more than a decade ago, had been the pastor of a sizeable Baptist church in Mount Pleasant. She lived alone, and was no longer able to take care of the big house by herself, and had a maid who came in to help her at least twice a week. The yard and handyman work was done by Ned.

Elaine wished that Ned hadn't left. She loved her grandmother, and had always enjoyed talking with her, but she knew that Mrs. Perdreau would ask her about herself and how she had been doing, and that was a subject Elaine wished to avoid. Ned was more fun to be around, and if he got too inquisitive, she could simply tell him to mind his own business. Besides, he was never serious about anything.

After supper Elaine pretended to have a headache. She went to her bedroom and read a book until she fell asleep.

Carolina Twilight

Ned was a year older than Elaine. A distant relation, he had been adopted as an infant by Mrs. Perdreau's older son and daughter-in-law after his parents were killed in an automobile accident. The couple had no children of their own, and Ned grew up an only child, idolized by parents who believed him to be something of a genius. They lived on the same family land, in a newer ranch style home about a mile from his grandmother's house, so naturally Mrs. Perdreau saw more of him than any of her other grandchildren and helped to raise him (sometimes administering spankings, of which Ned's mother disapproved).

As a little boy he had been somewhat spoiled and domineering with other children, and perhaps for that reason, Ned had always brought out the tomboy in Elaine. She remembered their childhood days together as both carefree and contentious. They had a lot of fun together, but there were also numerous conflicts and breaches, since she could be as willful as he was. When they grew older, the hostilities eased and became more playful and facetious.

Ned's father died of cancer when he was sixteen, and Elaine heard that he had gone through a rough time afterwards, nearly worrying his mother to death for a couple of years with wild misbehavior and disreputable friends. But somehow he had survived this difficult period, and, much to the relief of his family, he settled down and began working and making good grades in school again. Seeing Ned for the first time in several years, Elaine discerned no changes in him except for physical ones; he seemed to her his old silly self, only bigger and taller. Like a horse now, she thought, unconsciously taking on her grandmother's way of referring to the children as "horses" when they got to a certain size and unmanageability.

The next morning's breakfast was more lavish and appealing than the morning meal which was usually served at home, but Elaine ate only sparingly, not having much appetite. Her parents wanted to do some sightseeing and shopping in Charleston, but Elaine didn't go with them, as much as she loved the old city. She preferred Ned's company, and he had promised to come over. Mr. and Mrs. Perdreau helped the elder Mrs. Perdreau clean up after breakfast and then left for the day. Elaine grew impatient for Ned to arrive, fearing that her chit chat with her grandmother would turn too personal. Luckily, the telephone rang, and she took the opportunity to leave the house while Mrs. Perdreau was engaged in conversation with her sister Elizabeth.

Elaine walked out to the back porch, where the sight of an elegant white bird in the distance caught her attention. At the edge of the marsh, a tall white egret stood motionless on its black stilts like a statue, his long neck crooked gracefully and expectantly, his yellow eyes fixed on some spot in the waters nearby. Elaine watched him until he walked behind a tree and was out of sight.

She heard the sound of heavy footsteps inside the house, and as she turned around, heard Ned say, "Aha! Gotcha!"

A moment later he walked through the open doorway holding a kitten in each hand.

"Here you are, Elaine! Mind if I join you?"

"Sure," she answered, glad for his company.

She sat down on the porch swing, and he plopped down beside her and queried, "Kitten?" as though offering a cigarette or a drink, and handed her one.

"How did it go last night with your friend's move?" she asked.

Ned sputtered in disgust, "Don't ask. Nick was supposed to have everything packed and ready to go, but that guy was nowhere near ready when I got there. And it took way longer than—youch!"

Ned extracted the kitten's claws from the sensitive flesh of his bare inner thigh and gave her to Elaine.

"Here, let 'em maul each other. I think they're rabid."

"Aww, they're not," she protested, cuddling the tiny cats to her face.

"You better watch those fuzzy little fiends. Their daddy is half wild, and one mean son of a kitty cat."

She laughed and told Ned he was crazy. It was the first time she had really laughed in a long while.

He asked her about her brother Glen.

"Oh, he's great. He's always great."

"Do I detect a little sibling hostility there?"

"Oh, no!"

"Why didn't he come with you on this trip?" asked Ned.

"New girlfriend. Very serious."

"Ah!"

Their conversation naturally turned to reminiscences, and they talked with ease and familiarity. The two of them had spent many a summer and weekend together, and even after long separations had always been able to instantly resume their relationship of banter, friendly rivalry, and a concealed, almost grudging affection for each other. This time, nothing had changed in that respect, but there was a difference. The difference was in Elaine, of course, though she was doing her best to hide it from Ned.

Certain memories he recalled made her smile; she even laughed a few more times. They let the kittens go to play on the porch.

"Yes, I remember when you were a skinny little kid I could beat at arm wrestling," she retorted to a boast he made about some childhood feat.

"Once, maybe," he said with a scornful laugh, "when I was convalescing from a near fatal illness."

"I don't remember you having any such illness."

He drew one leg up onto the swing and propped a lean, muscular arm on his knee.

"Do you remember that little friend of yours named Diane?" he asked. "On a visit here, when I was in the sixth grade, I think, you showed me her school picture, and I developed a terrible crush on her. I even wrote her a letter that she never answered."

"Yeah, she asked me about you when you wrote to her," recalled Elaine. "I told her you had two heads."

"I figured you were working against me!" he laughed.

From the back porch they could see the little old farmhouse which sat a few hundred yards away from the big house, farther back from the water. She and Ned had sometimes gone exploring in it when they were younger, and Elaine wanted to see if all the interesting stuff she remembered was still inside, so they walked over. The old place had been uninhabited for many decades and was only used for storage now.

The house's exterior was clapboard painted a bluish green, and the high, hipped roof was clad with rusty tin. Azalea bushes dotted the front side of the house, and clumps of ivy grew between them and sent its vines up and over the red bricks of the front steps.

The screened porch was filled with miscellaneous junk: a broken rocker, buckets, pans, planters, vases, hoes, tools, and a rusted chest freezer. From here they entered into the main room, where there was a boarded-up fireplace to the left and a small kitchen to the right. The kitchen had a checkerboard pattern tile floor of green and gray, and the walls were painted green. A hot water heater stood in one corner, and in another was a vintage General Electric stove with push-button controls and a chrome clock that rose up over the center of the cooktop. The walls and ceiling of the living room, or main room, were covered with paneling painted a pastel rose. The floors were of a dark hardwood. The house had two small bedrooms, and off of one was a tiny bathroom in which there was a toilet and a bathtub only about two-thirds the size of a modern tub. The sink and a metal medicine cabinet were not in the bathroom, but tucked into a corner in one of the bedrooms.

All the rooms of the house were filled with furniture — bedsteads, baby beds, tables, chairs, chests — and in between and on top of the furniture, all manner of interesting stuff through which Elaine had enjoyed rummaging as a child — old records, religious and secular books, paintings, mirrors, mattresses, boxes, newspapers, kerosene heaters, pillows, lamps, rugs, trunks, and a phonograph player in a mahogany case. Elaine opened one trunk and found it full of magazines and books, including *Songs of the Gilded Age*, *The Jungle Book*, and a Baptist hymnal copyrighted 1916.

Ned reminded her how he had once come across a trunk containing old family papers dating back to the early 1700s. When his Aunt Elizabeth found out about it, she had immediately removed them, aghast that these valuable documents had been hidden away for decades in a leaky house without air conditioning, but elated that they had not been destroyed. The self-appointed keeper of the family archive, she added them to the family papers she already had, a collection of letters, diaries, plats, and other records of their Huguenot ancestors much coveted by the local historical society.

Elaine remembered now that Ned had told her about this

discovery when she was little. It must have been what gave her the idea that there was treasure in the place, and kept her on a quest for it whenever she visited her grandmother.

Finding no such treasure today, they eventually tired of their explorations and went back outside. It was beginning to rain. The skies had been bright and mostly blue only an hour before, and Elaine was surprised again at the quickness of weather changes in the South Carolina lowcountry. She had grown accustomed to the more predictable climate of middle Georgia, where skies brooded and darkened for hours before a thunderstorm, and then as slowly cleared afterwards. The lowcountry clouds seemed to race through the heavens, gather and rain, and then race out to sea or northward, leaving behind dazzling sunlight and the bluest of skies in a matter of minutes, propelled by the ever-present breezes off the water.

They ran to the big house and plopped down on the porch swing. The rain shower was light, and lasted less than half an hour.

"I need to check on my boat," said Ned.

They walked out to the dock, and Elaine paused at the edge of the yard to watch a minor spectacle going on at the narrow shore. It was low tide, and the receding waters had revealed the muddy, sandy bottom of the creek, which formed a beach marked by thousands of tiny holes. The mud crawled with life until Ned and Elaine appeared, but they remained still and quiet, and soon the multitude of strange little crabs cautiously emerged from the sand again and resumed their feeding. The males were distinguished by one monstrous claw much larger than the other which they held out crooked as one might hold out an arm offered to a lady. Ned's foot slipped on the wet grass, and his movement sent all the fiddler crabs scuttling sidewise back into their holes. But once again they returned, and, remaining near their tunnels, they moved about slowly picking up particles of food with their tiny, delicate pincers and putting them into their quickly opening and closing mouths.

Elaine followed Ned out onto the dock. He checked the lines to his sailboat and bailed out a small amount of rain water. It was a small craft, hardly big enough for two people.

"Want to take her out?" he asked Elaine.

"Not today."

He clambered back up on the dock via a rickety ladder.

"I'm hungry," he said. "How 'bout you?"

She shrugged indifferently. Ned offered to race her to the kitchen door, and took off running, but Elaine ambled behind him at her usual leisurely pace, and he gave up the idea, walking in stride with her when she caught up with him.

In the kitchen Ned opened the refrigerator and surveyed its contents briefly before settling on some leftover macaroni and cheese. He spooned some out into a bowl and began eating it cold.

"Want some?" he asked, nodding toward the larger bowl containing the rest of the concoction.

"Ugh." Elaine shook her head. "You eat it cold?"

"It's good! Homemade, you know."

Peanut, an elderly Chihuahua, was curled up on folded towels in a basket next to the refrigerator. Ned accidentally dropped some macaroni on the floor near the dog's bed, and when he reached down to pick it up, the shivering little canine bared his teeth viciously and made a strange, high-pitched growl.

"He still doesn't like you, huh?" Elaine observed.

"Nope."

"Imagine that, an animal not liking Dr. Doolittle."

"Actually, Mr. P doesn't like anyone, except Grandma, but he hates my guts."

"No, really?"

"Well, I did send him for a thrilling ride in the clothesline bag once when I was younger and meaner."

"That'll do it," said Elaine.

"He bit me once when I was a toddler. After that, we were mortal enemies. Grandma would switch me if I touched him, so I started playing mind games with the popeyed pipsqueak. At one time I had him convinced that he was being stalked by a Bolivian assassin."

"You're crazy."

A large ginger tabby cat strolled into the kitchen, curling his long tail around the door jamb as he passed by. She remembered this pet, her grandmother's favorite, as the biggest cat she had ever seen. His name was Claude, but that was just something written on a file at the veterinarian's office. No one in the family ever called him by this official name. To Ned he was known variously as "kitty bag," "kitty schmitty," "kitty smacker," "kitty poo," "kitty rascal," "muchie puchie," "puchie woochie," and a dozen other epithets— but never Claude. The animal wouldn't have recognized the name. Mrs. Perdreau referred to Claude as such only to differentiate him from her other cats when talking about them, but always addressed all her cats individually as merely "kitty."

"All cats are named kitty," she would say.

Ned reached down to pick up Claude.

"Come here, fat boy," he said. But, despite his size and advanced age, the chubby ginger cat leapt over his cupped hands like an acrobat jumping through a hoop and went over to his empty food dish. There he sat down and looked up at Ned expectantly, emitting one squeaky mew. Elaine saw a bag of dry cat food nearby and scooped out a handful for him.

Mrs. Perdreau walked in at that moment.

"Is that cat begging for food again? I just fed him," she said.

Elaine apologized.

"Oh, dear, that's all right! He's always overeating."

Mrs. Perdreau gave Elaine a hug and a kiss, and walked over to Ned and took his arm.

"Well, Elaine, what do you think of my handsome grandson? Isn't he something?"

It was plain she adored Ned, who had assumed a comical muscle man pose at her compliment.

"He's something, all right," Elaine replied with pointed sarcasm. Privately, she could not quite agree with her grandmother's description of Ned as 'handsome,' although he had an undeniably appealing, honest mug.

"Did you hear that?" he complained to Mrs. Perdreau, pretending to take shocked, petulant offense at Elaine's remark.

"Oh, Ned, act your age," she laughed, reaching up to muss his hair.

Mrs. Perdreau began some preparations for the evening's meal, and Ned and Elaine wandered outside again.

"Let's walk over to my house," he suggested. They did.

The brick ranch house where Ned lived looked a little out of place in its rural setting. Though it was surrounded by dense woods, the small front lawn was as perfect as any in suburbia, and a beautiful blue swimming pool sparkled in the back yard. Inside, Ned's mother kept an immaculate house. She had recently redecorated, and all the rooms were neat and clean and smelled of flowers — every room except Ned's, of course, which was a cluttered mess, and scented by a half-eaten bag of boiled peanuts that lay open on his dresser.

For Elaine, looking into her cousin's room had always been like peering into the weird whirlwind of enthusiasms and whimsy that was the mind and soul of Ned. The present population of animal life here now consisted of a few tropical fish in a small aquarium, but he had always loved animals of all kinds, and, in addition to the mandatory dog, Elaine remembered that he was never without at least two or three hamsters, snakes, fish, mice, lizards, turtles, or other small creatures in a cage or a tank. Once he had even raised a baby raccoon. As a child, he would have kept an entire menagerie in his room had his parents allowed it.

Ned had gone through countless phases of career aspiration, and his room still exhibited traces of many of them, from cartoonist to ventriloquist, astronaut to marine biologist, jet pilot to brain surgeon. Books, magazines and papers lay in jumbles on the floor and nearly every surface, and the walls were lined with a number of posters, including an element chart, images of the first moon landing, and pictures of W.C. Fields, Laurel and Hardy, and Johann Sebastian Bach. A Charlie McCarthy dummy was propped up in one corner on top of a speaker, and dusty plastic models of rockets and aircraft hung from the ceiling by fishing lines. The only oasis of order was found on his bedside table, where a reading lamp, a Bible, and a telephone were neatly arranged.

"Ned, you are such a slob!" Elaine remarked, looking around.

Ned looked around, too, as if through her eyes, and felt a little embarrassed.

"I should get rid of some of this junk. A lot of this stuff goes back a long way. I guess I don't even notice it anymore."

"And you need a bookcase in here. Why don't you get a bookcase, or some shelves?"

"Yeah, you're right."

Ned began to pick up some dirty clothes and put them in a hamper. Elaine picked up a high school annual from his senior year and thumbed through it. A number of pages were filled with inscriptions in different handwriting and inks, sentiments such as "To Ned Perdreau, a great mind warped by the over-consumption of Looney Tunes and moon pies. Have a great summer!" and "You've been a great friend. Don't ever change! I know you'll make a fine veterinarian, and fix my cats for free! God bless!"

On a cork bulletin board above a desk Elaine saw one of her wallet size school pictures from the fifth grade. She went over to it to get a better view. As she gazed at the smiling, pixie-faced girl with big brown eyes, she couldn't quite recognize this pert little spirit as herself. She tried to remember what it had been like to be that age, but found that she didn't know this little girl anymore.

Elaine turned away from the pictures and began to inspect Ned's record collection. Many of his albums were classical.

"Do you like classical music?" he asked her.

"I love it. Who's your favorite?"

"Bach, of course."

"Of course!" she responded absently, eyeing a guitar that stood in a corner next to his stereo.

"Are you going to favor us with a song or two while we're here?" she asked.

"Sure, later. Say, would you like to meet Buddy?"

"Who's Buddy?"

"My dog."

On their way out Ned paused on the back porch to show Elaine his telescope, a large, expensive-looking instrument on a tripod.

"You like to stargaze, don't you?" he asked.

"Yeah, but I don't have a telescope. I just like to sit up on the roof and look at the sky."

"On the next clear night we'll take this baby outside and I'll show you some neat stuff."

"Okay, sounds fun."

They walked out into a fenced section of the back yard, where a big black dog which looked to be part Labrador retriever immediately ran up to Ned and all but jumped up into his arms. Ned grabbed the adoring, ungainly animal and held the dog's face to his own while avoiding the slavering tongue at his chin.

"My son! My son!" he cried dramatically.

The dog squirmed out of his grasp and ran over to Elaine, jumping up and nearly throwing her off balance.

"Buddy!" Ned scolded, taking hold of his collar. "You think this dog needs pep pills?"

"He needs tranquilizers," replied Elaine, as she brushed some dirt off her clothes. "That's okay, Buddy," she added, petting him.

"He's a good dog, just a little too enthusiastic. He'll calm down when he gets older. He's not even a year old yet."

"Where did you get him?"

"I found him on the side of the road one day. There was this little black puppy just sitting there looking pitiful, so I had to bring him home."

"Of course you did," Elaine agreed.

At his feet Ned noticed what was left of a stuffed animal—a dog toy in the shape of a squirrel. He picked it up, and holding up the limp piece of fur high in the air as Buddy danced about and waited for him to throw it, he cried out in a sad, goofy voice, "I used to have a little friend, but he don't move no more."

Elaine couldn't help but laugh.

Buddy came along when they left the yard and walked back to

their grandmother's place. They found themselves at the edge of the marsh again. A steady, pleasant breeze was blowing; Elaine could smell the ocean in it, and the pluff mud. They sat down at the end of the dock and let their legs dangle over the side. They watched the scores of little crabs instantly disappear when Buddy bounded out into the mud.

Ned had been talking about his college friends, but had not mentioned any girls yet, so Elaine asked him if he had a girlfriend.

"No, there's nobody right now," he said, looking out over the seemingly endless expanse of marsh grass. After a pause, he ventured a guess that Elaine must have lots of boys interested in her.

She laughed, "Not even one, Ned."

"I find that hard to believe," he said, and, turning to her with a big smile, he added, "You sure are good looking these days."

Elaine smiled in embarrassment and looked away, but didn't really take his compliment as sincere. She wondered if Ned was feeling sorry for her, and defused the awkwardness of the moment with a sarcastic retort.

"Too bad I can't say the same about you."

He reacted with simulated agony, as though someone had stabbed him in the heart.

Chapter Ten

That evening, when Elaine's parents returned, everyone went over to Ned's house for supper. He was more serious in their company, less talkative at first, and even a little shy. Dr. Perdreau began to question him about the courses he was taking at college, and about his instructors, and the conversation split into two—one between himself and Ned, and the other between Adele and Mrs. Perdreau—while Elaine sat looking bored, showing interest only now and then, and only in what Ned was saying.

After the meal Ned's mother took them on a tour of her house and described her recent redecorating project. When they came to Ned's room she simply rolled her eyes, remarking, "I was not allowed to redo anything in this chamber of horrors. I suppose it would have been futile, anyway."

Dr. Perdreau noticed a guitar propped in a corner and asked Ned if he would favor them with a certain song. The tune he requested was the first one Ned had ever learned to play, and everyone remembered how, as a young boy, he would play it over and over again almost maddeningly.

"Oh, no, not that song!" laughed his mother.

"Have you increased your repertoire, Ned?" asked Dr. Perdreau teasingly.

"Why, I've almost tripled it!" he replied impressively.

His mother shook his shoulders playfully.

"Ned's just being silly," she told them. "He's really an excellent musician."

When the adults went on to see the rest of the house Elaine stayed behind with Ned in his room. They listened to records while she perused his scattered collection of books and music. Getting nosier, she just beginning to check out his closet and a collection of old comic books when Ned's mother popped her head in and asked him to come outside and play his guitar.

Ned reluctantly took it out to the porch, where everyone was seated, and Elaine followed. He sat down on a wicker ottoman, plucked a few strings, tuning them, and then launched into a beautiful piece of classical Spanish guitar music. He played skillfully, and Elaine and her parents were impressed. Ned's grandmother applauded him proudly. They persuaded him to entertain with one more selection, so he played and sang a spirited rendition of "I Fought the Law," knocking on the wood of his guitar to add the gunshot sound effects.

Crickets and cicadas supplied the music for the rest of the evening. The conversation waxed and waned on the porch as night slowly fell, while overhead, in a clear, indigo sky, the stars appeared and imperceptibly multiplied.

*   *   *   *   *   *

Ned had to work the next day, and didn't come over to his grandmother's house until just before dark. He found everyone in the dining room enjoying a feast of takeout Chinese food Elaine's parents had supplied. Famished, he sat down and filled his paper plate with pepper steak and fried rice. After a couple of large helpings he became talkative and got everybody laughing with a barrage of terrible jokes.

"Do ya'll know why tigers won't eat clowns?" he asked, forking an eggroll on his plate.

"I don't know," his mother played along. "Why won't tigers eat clowns?"

"Because they taste funny."

His audience groaned, but laughed anyway.

Elaine was not eating much. No one seemed to take notice, but Ned was aware of it. He had also noticed the unmistakable, inordinate sadness in her eyes and expression at times, most obvious when she thought no one was paying attention.

After a dessert of ice cream, the adults went out to the porch again to sit and converse. Elaine and Ned cleared off the table and put away the leftovers. He asked her what she wanted to do. She had been bored all day without him, and thought that they might go into town for a movie, but he looked a little tired, so she didn't suggest it. They wound up in the living room in front of the television set. Claude the cat joined them on the couch and groomed himself until he fell asleep next to Ned.

The movie on TV interested Ned, but Elaine was restless, and thinking of other things, dreading the upcoming trip to the mountains with her parents. She sighed and leaned back against the overstuffed arm of the sofa. Yawning, she carelessly kicked off her sandals, lifted her legs and tossed them over Ned's lap.

It had been a warm day, and she was wearing shorts. Ned looked down at the pair of shapely bare legs in his lap with a kind of stunned mortification, his face turning red. In the darkened room, Elaine didn't see his expression.

"Get those big old horse legs off me!" he huffed, abruptly pushing her off himself.

Elaine responded with a swift kick to his shin. Had they been younger, a wrestling match might have ensued, but Ned informed her she had gotten too "big and dangerous" to fight anymore.

"You think I'm fat?" she asked, insulted.

"No, actually, you're kind of skinny compared to the last time I saw you. You don't eat much, do you?"

She ignored the question.

When the movie ended Elaine walked outside with Ned. His mother had already gone home, and everyone else had retired to their rooms. They leaned against his car and lingered there for a while talking. The front porch light had not been switched on as usual, and the only light in the yard came from the dim yellow glow of the upstairs bedrooms.

"I was going to ask you if you wanted to stick around here for a while instead of going to the mountains with your parents," he said. "I could get some days off from work, and we could…"

The sentence was left unfinished.

"What?" she prodded.

"Oh, just have some fun. Go to the beach, you know, that sort of thing. You don't seem too excited about going to North Carolina."

"I'm not."

"Well, think about it, then," he suggested.

"I will."

Ned told her about a party to which he had been invited. He

asked her if she'd like to go with him, not seeing the look of alarm her face assumed momentarily.

"I'm not much for parties," she quickly replied. To Elaine, a party, or any kind of gathering, was just a place where her misery, awkwardness, and self-doubts were put on painful display for others.

Ned's disappointment with her answer was obvious. After a silence he asked, "Want to go to the beach tomorrow afternoon? I have to play for a soloist at church in the morning service, but I'm free the rest of the day."

"Sure, the beach sounds fine."

"You're welcome to come with us to church," he suggested.

"Mmm, maybe," she said, though she had no intention of going.

She rested her head against the curving roof of the car and gazed up a black sky full of stars. Ned looked up, too, and pointed out a few constellations. His brief lecture ended when Elaine broke into a huge yawn. Ned smiled and asked her if she was ready to go inside.

"I'm sorry," she apologized. "I didn't mean to interrupt."

He made a mock weary, dismissive gesture at the sky, sighing, "Eh, I get so bored with these vast universes."

Elaine laughed. He walked her to the door, where she lingered for a while, watching the lights of his car grow smaller as they moved farther away, and wondering why he drove ever so slowly down the familiar dirt driveway.

*   *   *   *   *   *

The next morning Elaine opened her eyes in the little bedroom to a morning fully broken, surprised that she had slept so late, or slept at all. It had rained briefly but heavily during the early morning hours, and for a while she lay in her bed gazing at the upper panes of the window above the white café curtains. The rain clouds had emptied themselves, and the sky was lit with a grayish, milky light so uniform and pure, that it was easy to imagine that if she were to draw back the curtains she would see only an infinite nothingness, nothing but this milky light, and not the familiar scene of the trees and the yard.

As she was stretching her arms she heard the sound of something, perhaps a pebble, hitting the screen of the half-open window just above her head. She sat up, parted the curtains, and looked out. Ned was standing a few yards from the house getting ready to toss another acorn her way. He was dressed in a dark brown suit and tie.

"Don't you look snazzy," she greeted him, opening the window.

"Thanks. Sleep well?" he asked. Tossing away the acorn and plunging his hands into his pockets, he walked toward the window.

"I slept all right."

"I didn't wake you, did I?"

"Weren't you trying to?"

"Well, I was just going to throw a few little objects at your window to see if you were already up. That was my plan."

"I see. And if I were up, what then?"

"Well, let me think...oh yeah, I was going to ask you if you wanted to go somewhere with me today."

"Where?" she asked.

"Anywhere you want."

"So, I can go anywhere I want..."

He nodded slowly.

"But I have to go with you."

"That's the catch, yeah."

They smiled at each other. She was resting her chin on the window sill, looking at him through the screen.

"Well—all right," she drawled, but suddenly raised her head and turned around. Her mother had opened the door of the bedroom and was looking in. When Mrs. Perdreau caught a glimpse of Ned outside she opened her mouth in a smile and then suppressed it.

"Breakfast is ready," she announced, and closed the door.

"Decide where you'd like to go," said Ned. "I'll see you when we get back from church."

"Okay."

Ned reappeared at the house after lunch, but just in time to grab a sandwich and some coleslaw as things were being put away in the kitchen. Elaine had not come up with any ideas about where they might go that afternoon.

"Let's just drive around," he suggested. "It's a nice day."

The top was down on his old convertible; the weather was warm, the sky completely clear. As they turned on to the highway she turned on the radio. An old song they both liked came on, and they sang along loudly. Ned drove by the nursery where he worked, slowing down and pointing out things with ostentatious, sweeping gestures. Elaine marveled, playing along. They drove over the larger, three-lane bridge over the Cooper River into the city, the winds whipping their hair about madly on the high spans.

Elaine loved beautiful things, so she loved old Charleston. She knew the streets and narrow lanes of the peninsula, and had spent many hours roaming them with cousins who lived downtown. Having worked some summers as a tour guide, Ned regaled her with a series of historical narratives as they drove around sightseeing. He pretended to be savvy about architecture, differentiating the various styles and details of the old homes they passed, but Elaine knew enough about the subject to scoff at such absurdities as "flying pilasters" and "corseted buttresses."

On their way out of the city, as they were waiting at a red light, a young man in an expensive-looking foreign sports car pulled up beside Ned and grinned at him in recognition. He was an old friend whom Ned hadn't seen in a long while, and they talked until the light changed. Elaine was briefly introduced and received a wink. When the cars began moving again the sports car zoomed off and left all the others behind. It had almost disappeared around a bend by the time Ned was cruising along in fourth gear again.

"What do you think?" he asked, peering at the car until it was out of sight.

"Of what?" asked Elaine.

"That car."

"It's cute," she responded negligently.

"You must be a real auto fanatic," he joked.

"Are you?" she asked curiously.

"I guess I used to be, because most of my best friends in high school were, like that gentleman you just met. That car of his—"

Ned suddenly paused with a thoughtful expression.

"You know," he said, "I just remembered, I let that guy borrow some tools from me a long time ago and I haven't seen them since. Man! I'll never get them back now... I guess I should have remembered Polonius's advice to Laertes—neither a borrower nor a lender be—or was it Laertes' advice to Polonius—or Benjamin Franklin?"

And he looked to her with ridiculous puzzlement.

"What about that car of his?" Elaine asked, ignoring his

nonsense.

"It used to be mine," he said.

"Really? How could you afford it?"

"Not very well, believe me. I didn't have it too long before I sold it to Jack. His parents are well off, and he usually gets what he wants. He's actually a pretty nice guy, pretty steady compared to some of the kids I knew. He was just sort of — reckless — a car and sports nut. He loved hunting and guns, and got me interested, too. I still do some target shooting, you know."

"You've got a gun?" she asked, fixing her eyes on Ned with such intensity for a moment that he thought she must have some extreme fear or hatred of firearms.

"A pistol," he replied hesitantly.

"Oh," she murmured, looking away. "No, I didn't know... you did target shooting."

The thought of a gun suddenly absorbed her. Ned had a gun. A gun! Elaine could hardly believe her luck. She could almost feel a great burden sliding off her shoulders. She felt free, and experienced an exhilaration that was almost like happiness. Changing the subject, she eventually steered the conversation to the matter of Ned's invitation.

"You know," she said, "I think I would like to stay here instead of going to the mountains with my parents. I'll ask them tonight."

Ned was very pleased. He asked her if she wanted to drive out to the islands to go for a walk on the beach. She really only wanted to go back to Ned's house to see this gun for herself, but agreed to a stroll on Sullivan's Island first.

Later, on the way home, she told Ned she'd like to listen to some of his record albums again. He was happy to oblige, and took her to his house. When they walked in to his room, Elaine was surprised to find it more orderly and clean than before. Ned admitted that having guests over had shamed into cleaning up a bit.

"What would you like to hear?" he asked, kneeling in front of the record collection near the stereo.

She looked over the classical music albums and picked out one at random.

"Some great selections on this one," Ned remarked. "I'll play you my favorite first—or was there a particular one you wanted to hear?"

"No, that's fine," she said absently, looking around the room.

He put the record on to play, and they sat down on the carpet in front of the stereo. They were alone in the house.

The music began. Ned reclined on the floor with his head behind his hands and closed his eyes. Elaine had spotted on top of a chest of drawers a wooden box which she thought might be a gun case. She was impatient to look, but, not wishing to reveal any interest in the pistol, she waited. After about a quarter of an hour passed, Ned sat up to change the record, but as soon as he lay down again the telephone rang, and he excused himself and went into another room to answer it.

Elaine got up from the floor cautiously and turned down the volume on the stereo a little. The call was for Ned; she heard him talking about work. She went over to the chest of drawers, pulled the wooden box toward her, and opened it. A pistol was inside, and beside it a small box of ammunition.

She simply looked at the gun for a while, but as Ned kept talking in the other room, she took it out of the case and slowly brought it to the side of her head. Her hand began to tremble slightly as she put her finger to the trigger. She even let the cold barrel of the gun lightly touch her temple. Feeling almost faint with fear, she put the gun back in its place and closed the box. She gave a start when she thought she heard Ned coming back. She froze, listened intently, and finally heard his voice again. The music selection ended, and in the silence before another piece began she heard him saying goodbye. She pushed the box back to its original position.

Elaine had just turned around, and was facing the door, when Ned came in and saw her.

He stopped just inside the doorway with an expression of mild alarm.

"Elaine, you're as pale as a ghost."

She put her hand against her cheek.

"Am I?"

There was a slight quaver in her voice.

"I must have stood up too fast."

Ned walked over to her, looking concerned.

"I have low blood pressure," she explained. "I feel faint sometimes."

She sat down on his bed, and the color soon returned to her face. Ned offered to fetch her some water or tea.

"I think I need to eat something," she said. "Okay if we go back to Grandma's?"

"Sure! You think you're all right, now?"

"I'm fine, I'm fine," she assured him, carefully getting to her feet.

On the short drive to Mrs. Perdreau's house he questioned her about her condition of low blood pressure, but she was vague and dismissed the matter as trivial.

"Don't worry," she said. "I get regular check-ups."

By the time they reached the house they were talking of other things, and Ned, who had the next day off, invited Elaine to go to the beach with him. She told him that she would.

At supper, her parents surprised her by announcing that they planned to leave for North Carolina the following morning. Time had flown on their visit, and Elaine didn't realize that it would be over so soon. She told her mother and father about Ned's invitation and asked if she could stay with her cousin and grandmother instead. Mrs. Perdreau made no objections; she suspected there was a budding romance between Elaine and Ned and wished to help it along. Dr. Perdreau said no at first; he didn't want to have to come back Charleston to pick her up on the way back, but Ned offered to drive Elaine home, or meet them somewhere along their return trip to Georgia, and eventually he gave in.

Early the next morning, Elaine said goodbye to her parents without showing much emotion, though she was inwardly grieved, believing that this was the last time she would ever see them.

*   *   *   *   *   *

Ned showed up punctually at ten. Elaine was upstairs in the bathroom when he arrived, and saw his car from the window. After combing her hair and taking a quick look at herself in the mirror, she started downstairs. She was wearing a gauzy open blouse over a two-piece bathing suit.

Ned happened to be at the foot of the stairs, and when he saw her coming down, he put his hand to his heart and staggered back a few steps, crying, "Whoa!"

"Funny," she snapped, glaring at him in embarrassment.

Elaine ignored another remark by him and picked up a beach bag she had left hanging on the stair post. Mrs. Perdreau was outside working in the garden, and they stopped to talk with her for a few moments before they left. Ned embarrassed Elaine again by referring to her as a "love goddess" in front of their grandmother.

They drove out to the beach and spread their blankets out on the sand. It was breezy by the shore, but the day was unusually warm for May. It was as if summer had already arrived. They lazed in the sun a while. All Elaine wanted to do was sunbathe, but Ned finally got her into the waves, where he sported around her like a playful porpoise. The water was too cold for her, and they soon returned to their blankets.

Elaine lay silent for a while, her eyes closed, her face to the sky. Ned was on his stomach beside her, watching her from time to time, trying to think of the right way to open a serious conversation. His grandmother had talked with him privately about Elaine, and was concerned about her. They both agreed she seemed very unhappy, but didn't know how to approach her about it, or even if they should. Mrs. Perdreau wondered if it was just a passing adolescent moodiness, or if Elaine had been recently jilted by a boyfriend.

"Sorry," Ned murmured at last.

Elaine turned her face to his, squinting in the bright sunshine.

"For what?" she asked, puzzled.

"For … embarrassing you at the house."

"Oh, that," she answered dismissively, turning her face back to the sun. "You're always embarrassing me. You're just an embarrassing person."

She put the back of her hand over her eyes with a long exhalation.

"Elaine," he said.

She waited, not answering, but fearing what he might bring up next by the serious tone of his voice.

But what he said next surprised them both. Ned found himself saying something he had meant to keep to himself—for a while, at least.

He blurted out that he was in love with her.

Elaine dropped her hand and looked over at him in astonishment. She could tell, from the look on his face and the way he hung his head and kept his eyes lowered, that he wasn't joking. A deep blush suffused his skin from the base of his neck to the roots of his hair. Even his ears were red.

She didn't know what to say. Ned glanced at her, saw the surprise and disbelief on her face, and smiled a little. He propped himself up on his elbows, sighed, and asked her how she felt about him, still red as a beet.

Elaine answered very carefully, having no wish to hurt his feelings.

"You know I've always loved you, Ned."

His head slipped down a notch. "But you don't feel the same way I do..."

"No."

He said nothing for a long while. Elaine studied his crestfallen expression with fading disbelief, and sadness. She told Ned he didn't really know her.

At this he turned on his side and faced her, propping his head in one hand, and asked her, with an openly affectionate look and a smile, "What don't I know?"

"Lots of things."

"Tell me, then."

Elaine would not—though she was tempted. She wanted to confide in Ned, but knew that it wouldn't do any good, and might do her harm. She wanted nothing interfering with her plans now.

"Look, Elaine," he said earnestly, "There are probably some things you don't know about me which aren't so pretty."

"Oh, I heard about all that, how you went crazy after your dad died, but it really wasn't so bad, and it's all in the past. You're pretty much your old self now."

"I see."

Ned sighed and fell on his back, shading his eyes against the dazzling sun.

"So you're saying that if I knew all about you, I wouldn't love you?"

After waiting for an answer, he looked at her. She nodded.

"It must be something pretty bad," he said, suppressing a smile.

"It is."

"Are you a cannibal?" he asked, with immediate regret for his facetiousness.

Elaine's eyes narrowed in sullen irritation. Bitterness spilled out of her, against her better judgment.

"No, something worse," she said sardonically. "I'm a mental case."

Not sure if he should take her seriously, Ned replied with a tentative smile, "Well, so am I."

"But you don't mean that. I do."

"You seem all right to me, Elaine. Just unhappy."

She sat up and looked out at the ocean. Ned sat up, too, moving a little closer. She finally spoke up, quickly and matter-of-factly.

"I'm taking an antidepressant and a tranquilizer. I'm seeing a therapist, and I have been on and off ever since I was hospitalized not so long ago for three months in a private psychiatric hospital. Now, do you still think you know enough about me?"

It took him a moment to recover from his surprise.

"No, I didn't know all that, Elaine," he said. "But it doesn't change anything for me, and it doesn't mean you're a mental case just because you're depressed. I've been depressed before myself."

"Not like me."

He had no answer for this, but after a long silence he asked her quietly, "Can I tell you what I see when I look at you, Elaine?"

She pulled her legs up to her body and buried her face between her knees, making no response. He told her anyway.

"When I look at you I see an attractive, intelligent girl with a kind heart. You also have a great sense of humor, although that's kind of hidden away right now."

"That's just someone in your mind," she muttered.

"No, no. I don't think there's any fantasy in my mind, Elaine. I think there's a hobgoblin in yours."

She reared her head and flashed him a withering look.

"I'd like to go home now," she said, abruptly gathering up her things. "I'm getting sunburned."

Nothing more was said until they were in his car, halfway home. In his own thoughts Ned was berating himself for his stupidity and tactlessness. Elaine was keeping her face turned away from his, and when he finally caught a glimpse of her expression she looked angry. He apologized for what he had said at the beach, about the hobgoblin. She told him she wasn't angry, but after he apologized, the look disappeared.

The silence resumed, and Ned switched on the radio. Elaine was thinking about the gun and her plans to use it. The night before she had thought of nothing else, and kept seeing herself pulling the trigger, and falling, ending. She hoped to harden herself by rehearsing this image over and over again in her mind, and to some extent she succeeded. She was beginning to feel a kind of peace about it all now.

At Mrs. Perdreau's house they made some sandwiches and ate

them in the kitchen. Elaine glanced out the window by the table and saw Ned's dog trotting about the yard.

"How did he get loose?" Ned complained. Worried about the kittens, he called Buddy and confined him on the porch. The dog spotted a squirrel and began barking and pawing at the screen door.

"I better take him home before he tears up Grandma's screens. Want to come over?"

"Nah, I'll just stay here."

"Okay, I'll be right back."

Elaine finished a glass of lemonade on the porch. She noticed a large rope hammock stretched between two pine trees near the marsh, and when Ned returned, he found her sitting in it.

The seating for two was rather precarious; Ned tried not to crowd her when he climbed on, but, making a sudden movement, he nearly tipped them both out.

"Sorry," he laughed.

Elaine drew her legs up onto the hammock and stretched out on one side. Ned followed her example, and carefully lay down alongside her, resting his head at the opposite end, so that they faced each other. It was early afternoon when they went outside, and they lay in the hammock talking until it was nearly sunset.

Ned apologized repeatedly for his tactlessness. Elaine seemed to have already forgotten their earlier tiff, and told him not to worry about it. She seemed to be in a better mood, and smiled easily. Regretting her outburst at the beach, she tried to minimize it with some fabrications.

"Actually, Ned, I'm doing much better now. The medications have really helped, and the doctor says I can probably do without them soon."

"Really? That's great!"

"I guess I seem more depressed than usual because…"

She hesitated.

"What?' he asked.

"Well … it's a girl thing."

"Ah, beg your pardon," he said, looking abashed.

Figuring she could no longer use her emotional problems as an objection to a possible romantic relationship, he gingerly approached the subject of his feelings for her again, this time in a more lighthearted manner.

"Ned," she sighed, interrupting him, "I'm sorry, but I don't feel that way about you."

This was an objection he found harder to overcome, but he suggested that her feelings might change over time, if she would just gave him a chance.

"It's possible, isn't it?" he urged.

She had to admit that anything was possible.

"It's not like we're first or even second cousins or anything," he went on, "so you wouldn't have to worry about any two-headed children."

She laughed, protesting, "But we are kind of distantly related — by marriage or something — I forget."

"Yes, but you know, the Perdreaus always marry their cousins."

"Not anymore."

"Dern! Well, doesn't matter. So, what do you say? We could get married and have a pretty little girl who looks just like you, and a couple of mean little boys."

Elaine's mouth dropped open at his persistence about marriage and children.

"Ned!" she exclaimed. "You sure are jumping ahead of yourself!"

"It was just a suggestion," he said, shrugging and grinning broadly.

*   *   *   *   *   *

The next day, Ned had to work. Knowing this, Elaine stayed up late watching television, and slept late into the morning. This was the first time during her visit that she would be alone with her grandmother. To avoid any serious conversation, she was cheerful and chatty, and offered to help with chores. She helped Mrs. Perdreau put up some new curtains in her bedroom, worked alongside her in the garden, and after lunch did some raking on her own in the side yard.

In the late afternoon, she found her grandmother dusting in the den. Mrs. Perdreau began to ask Elaine about school and her career plans, but, after giving answers which were not true but only meant to please, she turned the conversation away from herself and asked about the interesting old photographs that filled the room.

"I know you've told me who they are, but I forget," said Elaine.

One of the photographs was a portrait of Mrs. Perdreau and her husband, taken just after their marriage in 1911. The focus was clear and sharp, the faces very pale, as though powdered white, with distinct features framed by dark hair against a sepia background. The young man, whose name was Will, wore a straw hat at a jaunty angle and a broad, puckish grin on his face. The young woman's expression was unsmiling but pleasant, and there was an intent look in her eyes. Husband and wife sat very close together, their faces turned toward each other slightly, and Mrs. Perdreau's delicate white hand rested on his shoulder. Elaine thought she looked beautiful, and said so. Her grandmother laughed softly and replied that she must have been very photogenic.

"You know, at first, my family didn't want me to marry Will," she reminisced, smiling. "He wasn't an Episcopalian! But he had Huguenot ancestors like my family, so they were all right with him. He was so charming and kind, they couldn't help but love him."

After looking at the framed pictures, Elaine picked up an old photo album. It had leather covers decorated with tinted floral designs. They sat down on the loveseat and began turning the pages, and Mrs. Perdreau named off the persons in the portraits, some of which were 18th century silhouettes. Now and then Elaine stole a glance at the mantel clock, although she found that she was more interested in the names and stories of her ancestors and relations than she had been in the past.

Elaine had been told much about her family history before, but had never paid much attention or attached much importance to it, and she knew that this distressed her grandmother, to whom such things were very important. Mrs. Perdreau knew intricate genealogies going back a number of generations. She had preserved images of many of these people, and seemed proud of most of them. Elaine had never felt any connection with them, but her grandmother did, and more than that, beyond her own family, it seemed that Mrs. Perdreau could trace a kind of spiritual connection and kinship going back through all the ages — back to the garden of Eden! A series of biblical engravings that hung on the walls, scenes from the Old Testament and the New, next to a painting of the persecuted Huguenots, attested to this lineage.

When they had finished with the first album Mrs. Perdreau brought out another, older one, with tintypes, daguerreotypes and other kinds of photographs that dated back into the middle of the nineteenth century. Elaine lost count of how many 'greats' went before this or that grandparent, uncle, or aunt, or how many times some cousin was removed. Some of the ladies were lovely, others fat, aged, or plain, or some combination thereof, while all the men seemed bewhiskered and serious. Many of them were ministers or doctors; the rest planters or businessmen. A few were soldiers or officers in gray.

"My sister Elizabeth has all the best military portraits in the family," said Mrs. Perdreau. "She put them on loan to a museum in Charleston, along with a few remnants of the family china. At her house, she also has older portraits, paintings, going back into the 1700s."

"I'd like to see those," said Elaine.

"Well, we'll have to go downtown one day and pay her a visit, then. She told me she wanted to see you while you were here."

As they turned another page in the album the telephone rang. Mrs. Perdreau answered it in the kitchen and came back in a moment.

"Ned may be a little late," she said. "He's having some car trouble. Why don't we go ahead and get supper started? If he's very late we'll just heat him up some leftovers."

As it turned out, Ned was not too late, but walked in just as Elaine and Mrs. Perdreau were sitting down to their meal. The car trouble had not been serious, only a dead battery. After chowing down on two helpings of delicious meatloaf, mashed potatoes, and vegetables, he announced that he had quit his job at the nursery.

"They wouldn't give me any more days off this week," he explained.

"Ned! You shouldn't have quit your job on my account!" Elaine scolded him.

"Don't worry about it! I liked working there, but I've got

another job lined up soon at a vet's office, and you know I prefer animals to plants. It'll be good experience for me, since I plan to go into that line myself."

"Well," said Mrs. Perdreau doubtfully, "you should have given them more notice, Ned."

"Uh, I did, a while back … sort of."

Chapter Eleven

Ned and Elaine drove into town that evening for a movie. The next day, Ned spent part of the morning doing some yard work he had promised his grandmother. Elaine helped, and Mrs. Perdreau brought out big glasses of ice water and lemonade to them as the day grew hotter. Later, Ned took Elaine out into the salt marsh creeks and inlets and beyond in his sailboat. As the afternoon waned, the gusty breezes on the open water grew chilly, and he headed back for the dock.

After supper, Elaine said that she was in the mood for a walk. Her secret aim in this was to find some excuse to stop by Ned's house again to see the gun. She wanted to reassure herself that it was still in the same place, available for her use, and very soon.

They wandered down the long driveway, heading toward the main road with no particular destination. Towards the end of the driveway Elaine noticed two well-worn ruts leading off into the woods, seemingly to nowhere. She asked about them.

"Oh, every now and then, the road to the church floods, and

they have to use this back way," he said, moving a large branch which had fallen on to the dirt drive.

"There's a church near here?"

"You've never seen it? It's a black congregation called Mount Zion. Come on, I'll show it to you. You can't see it from here."

They walked down the grassy ruts, which took a curve into the woods which obscured them, and eventually found themselves in a clearing. Atop a slight rise, Elaine saw a simple rectangular building of white clapboard. A low steeple rose over the front double doors, which were painted dark green like the shutters. The windows were adorned with multicolored panes of opaque glass. Cars were parked on the grass all around the church building, and Ned and Elaine began to hear voices from inside.

"Let's go," she said uncomfortably. "They're having a service."

"I forgot, it's Wednesday night."

There was a sudden explosion of music from the building, rich, full, and rhythmic. It sounded almost as though a full orchestra were playing. Elaine heard a piano, an organ, guitars, trumpets, and drums.

"I tell you," said Ned, listening, and looking impressed. "They've got great music here."

He began to nod his head with the rhythm.

"We really ought to go," Elaine urged. "We're trespassing."

"Oh, no. I know lots of the people who go here, and they know me. It's really pretty inside. They've got a mural behind the altar that's a sight to see. I'll show it to you."

"I'm not going in there!" she protested. "That would be rude!"

"We can just take a peek through the door."

"No!"

Ned spotted a wooden ladder propped up against the far end of the church building, next to a window that was partly open at the top.

"We can just go two or three steps up that ladder and peep in through the window, just for a second. Come on, Elaine! It's an adventure!"

"You're crazy," she said, but reluctantly followed him to the foot of the ladder. A single, piercing falsetto male voice was singing to the music now.

Ned climbed up just high enough to look over the top of the sash.

"Wow, this is great," he said.

Elaine tugged on one of his socks impatiently.

Suddenly, a tall, elderly black man appeared around the corner of the building and was instantly at the ladder. Elaine wilted in embarrassment as he glared at her for a moment and then yelled up at Ned.

"Ned Perdreau!" he cried indignantly. "What do you think you are doing, young man?"

Ned looked down at him with a sheepish attempt at a smile.

"He-e-ey, Mr. Manigault!" he quavered nervously.

"Get down from there!" the gentleman demanded.

Ned jumped down from the ladder to the ground.

"Now why on earth would you be peeping through the window here on a Wednesday night? Are you a peepin' Tom?"

The old man, a well-dressed deacon in a dark suit, shook with a mild palsy which Elaine mistook for extreme anger. The thick lens of his glasses, magnifiers of size and light, were filled with two unnaturally large, luminous brown eyes.

"Uh, no, sir, I just wanted to show my cousin Elaine here the mural in the church."

Mr. Manigault sniffed and threw his head back in disdain.

"You expect me to believe that? I know you were about to be up to some mischief. I'm gone speak to your grandmother about this."

"I'm telling you the truth, Mr. Manigault."

The deacon pursed his lips and knit his brows in consideration for a moment, then said, "Well, then, if you want to see the church, then you both come on inside with me."

He took hold of Ned's sleeve and made a movement toward the front doors.

"But Mr. Manigault—"

"Young man," said the deacon, with authority in his staccato diction, "you come on in with me or I will tell your grandmother about the last time I caught you here smoking a cigarette."

"That was a long time ago!"

"You come with me. I believe Pastor Bell will want to have a word with you."

Ned looked at Elaine in an odd way, shrugged in resignation, and let Mr. Manigault begin leading him toward the church. The deacon reached back and caught Elaine's sleeve, also. She followed along, trudging and rolling her eyes in exasperation.

The music burst forth in their ears as the doors opened, and Mr. Manigault directed Ned to a half-filled pew in the back of the church. Elaine slipped in beside him, and the deacon took a seat on the end to prevent any early departures. At the front of the church, a young man in a shiny blue suit was finishing up a fast-moving gospel tune, accompanied by all the instruments Ned and Elaine had heard outside. Most of the members of the congregation were on their feet clapping and dancing with the music. Few had noticed the two latecomers on the back pew; those who did looked mildly puzzled and curious, but smiled at Ned, who was soon clapping and enjoying the music, also. Elaine shrank into her seat and kept her head down.

When the music and the applause ended, everyone sat down. Elaine leaned over to Ned to say something, but, feeling Mr. Manigault's enormous eyes on her, she sat up straight again and decided to speak to him later.

The singer and the instrumentalists filed off the platform, and Elaine got a good look at the mural Ned had mentioned. It was impressive, though not extremely large, filling the just the top half of the wall above a paneled area. The mural depicted the resurrected Christ, a scene of triumph painted in a dynamic folk art style with lurid but beautiful colors.

A man led a prayer, then also left the platform as a dignified, elderly gentleman in a well-tailored suit, obviously the pastor, took his place at the pulpit. He was a rather ugly, slight man, almost skeletal, and his sparse hair was a mixture of gray and white. After lowering his head in a brief prayer, he stood very straight and somewhat stiffly and looked out on the congregation with a smile.

"Well, it's good to be back among you, brothers and sisters," he began, in a voice deep and resonant.

The pastor's flock welcomed him back with raised voices and spatters of applause.

"Yes," he said, nodding, "As you know, we went to visit my wife's family up north, and to do some sightseeing, too. Now a vacation is nice, and everybody needs one once in a while, but it is good to be back home. This evening, I am not going to continue our Bible study, but I am going to speak about something which happened to me recently. The Lord seemed to be saying to me that I ought to speak on this tonight."

A baby shrieked, and the pastor paused for a moment until the infant was quieted.

"Well friends, whenever my dear wife and I are on vacation, we like to visit the local church in the place we are visiting. There was a church near our motel, so we just decided to go there last Sunday morning. It was a white folks' church, but they welcomed us, yes, they welcomed us — as visitors."

A wave of low laughter briefly rippled across the congregation.

"And you might be interested to know, brothers and sisters, that it was a fine church, and that the pastor was a fine, handsome man like yours."

The congregation tittered and laughed loudly at this.

The preacher smiled broadly, and then went on more seriously, "Now the name of the sermon that morning, I noticed in the program, was 'The Lilies of the Valley,' and I thought to myself, and remarked to my wife beside me, that was a good text for a sermon, a very good lesson for the Lord's people."

The congregation uttered approving murmurs. Some heads nodded continuously in approbation of his every word.

"But do you know, my brothers and sisters, that preacher stood up there, and for thirty long minutes — I do not lie, my friends — that man stood up there and talked about how pretty flowers are."

The preacher paused and looked about the church in wide-eyed amazement and consternation.

"And from what I could gather, the point of the sermon was, that we should thank God for the flowers because they are lovely. When he finished that sermon, my mouth done drop open!"

The congregation shook their heads and made sounds and comments of disapproval.

"Well, my friends, as I was sitting there in the pew listening to this sermon, I noticed a young man sitting nearby, and he looked very upset about something. I don't know what. Maybe he had girlfriend problems. But he just looked very, very sad. I began thinking to myself, what if that boy is sitting there thinking about putting a gun to his head? What if he is thinking of taking his own life?"

As he paused again for a moment, Elaine felt the blood rushing out of her head. Ned was watching the emotional outburst of an elderly woman in the pew next to theirs, and didn't see her turning pale.

When the old woman quieted, the pastor continued, "And I wondered to myself, what if this young man came here to this church to make one last attempt to get help, or guidance, or something! And I thought, what if I was that boy, sitting there in despair, listening to this sermon about the lilies? What if I had come here seeking the bread and water of life, and they gave me nothing but a little old flower instead? What would I do when I left this place, when I had been planning to put a gun to my head before I came? Well, I tell you, if I was that boy, I would leave that church and walk out to the park where all the pretty flowers are, and then directly, I would put that gun to my head and pull that trigger. That's what I'd do."

Leaning forward over the pulpit, the old gentleman was fairly trembling with anger.

"Beloved! We've got people in the church that's hurting! We got people in the church and out of it that needs help! A wounded spirit who can bear? We got a whole world out there that needs the truth! And what did this fine-looking pastor give the poor hungry sheep? Flowers? Flowers!"

The preacher leaned back and gazed up at the ceiling, shaking his head. The congregation mirrored his frustration with murmurs and shaking heads.

He took a deep breath and went on in calmer voice, "Now it is true, my brothers and sisters, that God made the flowers, and made them pretty, too. The whole of creation declares its maker—the heavens declare the glory of God, amen? But that was not even this preacher's point. What good does it do a soul that is lost to hear about how pretty the flowers are? We have got people in the church and outside the church that are walking around in hell! We have got dead folks walking around. They in their own private hell, and when they die, they will be in a worse one with the Devil and his angels! They are in darkness! Lost! They need to know that God has made a way for poor, miserable sinners to be saved—the man Jesus Christ! Amen?"

The church resounded with a chorus of "Amens!" Many in the congregation jumped to their feet and clapped and shouted loudly in agreement.

"And when you are in hell, you know you are in hell, and that you are weak and wretched and in need of help. And you know you are going to die someday. You may not know for sure that there is a lake of fire waiting for you but you are not so sure there ain't one, neither. You do know, however, that you are in hell right now, that you are all messed up. What book tells you the truth? What book tells you the truth and nothing but? What book says, all have sinned, and fallen short of the glory of God? What books tells dead men how to get life?"

The pastor held up his Bible and waved it in the air.

"This book!" he cried.

The congregation exulted. After a period of exclamations and brief outbursts of song, they quieted, and the speaker continued.

"Well, some poor soul might say to me, Pastor, you are right. I am in hell, and I need help. But the problem is, I don't believe in God, so how's He gone help me? I would say to that poor soul, sinner, now, if you were out in the sea on a sinking lifeboat—no food nor water, and feeling weak and 'bout to die—and you looked off in the distance, and thought you saw a boat passing by, but you didn't know if it was real or if you were just seeing a mirage, or having a delusion, and didn't know if anyone was really there to hear you call for help, wouldn't you call out anyway? Wouldn't you call out, on the chance—just the chance—that somebody might hear you and save your life? And this sinner would say to me, Yes, Pastor, I suppose I would call out, even if I didn't know if that boat was really there or not. And I would say to this poor soul, and if somebody on that boat did hear you, and did throw you out a lifesaver, wouldn't you then believe that boat was real, and that there was someone really there who could hear you and help you? And that sinner would say to me, Yes, I would have to believe it then. Then I would say to him, even if you don't believe in the Lord, ask Him to help you, and see what happens. Amen? What is the text, brothers and sisters? Taste of the Lord, and see if He is good! Tell me this—just what have you got to lose? Say to the Lord, oh Lord, help my unbelief! That is a prayer God will honor!"

Another long period of amens, shouts, and spontaneous outbursts of singing and declamations of scripture followed. The pastor finally ended his sermon with a lengthy, fervent prayer, after which the musicians and the singer returned to the stage, closing the service with a reverent rendition of "Rock of Ages."

As the music was drawing to a close, a few people began trickling out of the church, but after the music ended most of them were still standing about inside conversing. Noticing that Mr. Manigault had left his seat to attend to some duty, Ned grabbed

Elaine's hand and took the opportunity to exit the building with her.

Outside, they walked quickly to the edge of the woods where the rutted driveway began. By now it was getting dark. Elaine quickened her pace even more and took one last look at the church, half expecting to see the troubling eyes of the deacon upon them.

When they were well away and concealed by the woods, Ned remarked, "Some service, huh?"

Elaine just shrugged. She had a stunned look, and he could tell that she was deep in thought about something.

"Have you ever been to a black church before?" he asked.

"No. Have you?" she responded absently.

"A couple of times. I guess it can be a kind of shock to your senses if you're not used to it, with all the shouting and the dancing."

"I guess…"

"Is something wrong, Elaine?" He had expected her to be angry with him for getting her into trouble at the church, but she was so preoccupied that she had not said a word about it.

"I—I think the loud music gave me a headache," she said, though she had no headache.

"I'm sorry," he apologized. "I shouldn't have taken you up to the church. I thought it would be fun, but it was really dumb of me to do that. I'm sorry. You're not mad at me, are you?"

"No, Ned. Let's just forget it."

They walked back to their grandmother's house, and Elaine used the excuse of the headache to part ways with Ned and go to her room. She had completely forgotten about going to his house to check on the gun.

She lay in her bed and stared up at the ceiling, thinking about the sermon. Her mind was still reeling from it. Was it only a coincidence, she asked herself, that this man had talked of putting a gun to one's head? Had those words been meant for her? She could hardly comprehend this, and yet something inside argued that it was so. Late that night, she fell asleep still wondering.

When Elaine woke up in the morning, the previous evening seemed very far away. She thought about the church service again, vacillated between belief and doubt, and finally decided that she couldn't know for sure.

Her course was set, and she was still on it.

*   *   *   *   *   *

At breakfast, while Mrs. Perdreau was working in her gardens in the cool of the morning, Ned told Elaine apologetically that he had a longstanding commitment to play his guitar at a special church concert that night, and that he would have to leave around six o'clock for it. He invited her, but she declined.

"Is your mother going?" she asked him, after a thoughtful pause.

"She usually goes to my concerts, but tonight she'll be at her sister's house. My aunt Laura had an operation this week, and Mom promised to stay with her a couple of days now that she's just out of the hospital."

"Is Grandma going?"

Slightly puzzled by her inquisitiveness, Ned answered, "I don't think so, but I'm sure she'd come if you did."

Elaine pretended that there had been a facetious purpose to her questions.

"Hmm," she said. "Your mother's not going, Grandmother's not going, and I'm not going. Looks like nobody's going. You're not very popular, are you?"

She managed a smirk, and Ned smiled blandly.

Over the morning meal, Elaine hardly heard what he was saying, though she pretended to listen to his plans for their day together. She was thinking of the opportunity which had presented itself just now. The absence of Ned and his mother was all she needed for access to his gun and the freedom to use it.

They drove into Charleston again, walked in the market and the historic district and lunched at a popular restaurant with a rooftop view. Ned didn't broach the subject of his feelings for her that day, but he frequently gazed at her with unconcealed affection, and put his arm around her once when they sat down to rest on a park bench.

Elaine was blithe and playful one moment, brooding the next. She felt peaceful and happy that she finally found the easy route of escape she had been seeking so long, but at times she was fearful and uneasy, thinking of the irrevocability of what she planned to do, and the grief that it would cause her family. Ned was troubled by her moodiness, but kept his concerns to himself for the present. He was surprised when Elaine showed no interest in paying a visit to her cousin Emily, who had been her best friend in childhood and still lived in an old Victorian house downtown.

Ned reluctantly dropped her off at their grandmother's house in the afternoon. He asked her one last time to come with him to the concert that night, but again she refused, making excuses.

"I'm tired," she said. "You wore me out today. After supper I'll probably just watch a little TV and go to bed early."

Her grandmother was napping when she went inside, and Elaine was relieved to have some time alone to think about her plans for that night, and to prepare.

Carolina Twilight

*   *   *   *   *   *

Elaine emptied her purse of nearly everything but a small wallet, and then, for no particular reason, she showered and changed her clothes. While she waited for nightfall, she lay in her bed and wondered if she ought to leave a note behind for her family. As she thought of things to write, her feelings overcame her, and finally burst forth in sobs she tried to muffle with a pillow.

She didn't hear the bedroom door open, but sat up abruptly when she heard her grandmother softly speak her name.

"I'm sorry not to knock," said Mrs. Perdreau, looking distressed, "but I thought I heard you crying. Please tell me, what's the matter, dear?"

"It's something personal, Grandma," Elaine answered, with a kind of wail in her voice. "I can't talk about it. Please leave me alone."

"It hurts me to see you so upset. Isn't there something—"

"Please! Grandma—it's nothing to do with you. I just really need to be alone now, please. I'll get over this myself."

"Well...," she murmured sadly, closing the door.

Now Elaine felt that she had to get out of the house, and away from her grandmother, before she somehow betrayed herself. Taking deep breaths, she calmed down, combed her hair and put on a little makeup to conceal the redness around her eyes. Before leaving she snuck out to the back porch and left her purse on the steps. She found Mrs. Perdreau in the kitchen making some tea. The tiny old dog Peanut was sitting at her feet, and for some reason, he growled at Elaine when she appeared.

Mrs. Perdreau looked up and saw her granddaughter's somber face.

"I'm going for a walk, Grandma," she said quietly.

Mrs. Perdreau nodded. She tried not to show her concern for Elaine, but couldn't help but say, "Please don't stay out after dark. It's almost dusk now."

"Oh, I'll be all right. I like to walk in the evening. If I'm not back by dark I'll be at Ned's house."

Elaine paused. She suddenly wanted to hug her grandmother, as a way of saying goodbye, but she didn't trust herself not to break down again, so she simply turned and walked away.

Chapter Twelve

Elaine quickened her pace when her grandmother's place was out of sight. From the moment she left the house, one bad memory after another had flowed into her mind, and she soon became wholly absorbed, lost, in a tormenting series of thoughts repeating itself over and over again. It was only when Ned's house came into view that she could clear her mind somewhat and concentrate on the present.

At the edge of the yard she stopped and looked around. No cars were in the driveway. Ned's dog barked at her ferociously, but soon recognized her and began to wag his tail. She hurried up to the front steps and took a house key out of its hiding place under a flower pot. She had seen Ned use it once when he had forgotten his keys.

Inside the house, she went directly to his room and found the gun case. She opened it, carefully took the gun out, along with a box of ammunition, and put both in her purse.

Before she went out she looked around the room a last time,

considering whether she should leave a note behind. On the bed there were some books and papers. She found a blank sheet and a pen, and sat down on the edge of the bed. Her head was bent over the paper a long time before the pen touched it, but she ended up writing only this: "I love you. Forgive me." She wanted to be sure that Ned wouldn't find the note too soon, and decided to put it in the gun case.

As she crossed the room again, the light of a fiery orange sun flashed in her eyes. She locked the front door behind her and returned the key to its hiding place.

Elaine walked at a brisk pace down the unpaved road, and for a while the western sky was before her. The sun had sunk behind flattened streaks of clouds which glowed with coppery and ruddy colors, tinting everything with a warm, golden glow. By the time she reached the end of the road the fiery horizon had faded into a pale watercolor of itself, and was giving way to the first gray wash of night.

She walked as fast as she could along the highway. Before long she could see the neon sign of a roadside motel far up ahead. Her thoughts began to wander, and random memories, bits of conversations, and fleeting images floated through her mind. She became conscious of a dull headache returning, and aching eyes that still felt swollen from her cry. At one point, fancying that she heard a car slowing down behind her on the highway, she stumbled and broke into a run, and kept running until she reached the motel.

In the parking lot she brought out the purse she had been hiding in her jacket and slung its strap over her shoulder. The desk clerk, a sullen middle-aged man, woke from a nap in his chair as she entered the office. Their conversation was minimal, and she paid for her room with cash.

When she closed and locked the door of her motel room she immediately fell on the bed with a sigh. There was suddenly a pressured feeling in her head, as though there were too much blood, and then a sharp stab of pain, after which her headache became much worse. Automatically she reached into her pocketbook for an aspirin tin—but she had to pull out the bulky gun and ammunition box first, placing them aside on the bed with an ironic grimace. There was a much quicker cure for her headache! But she wasn't quite ready. She took several aspirin and one of her tranquilizers to calm herself.

After her headache eased she went over to the window and looked out through the drapes. The sky was black now. She wondered if her grandmother was getting worried about her yet, and whether she had called Ned's house to check on her. A car suddenly pulled into the parking lot, startling her. She closed the curtains and went back to the bed.

She lay on her side with her head facing the gun and stared at it for a long time. The panic which had come over her earlier in the day was gone. She felt weak, but not so weak that she couldn't put the gun to her head and pull the trigger.

*   *   *   *   *   *

Mrs. Perdreau telephoned Ned's house when Elaine wasn't home by dark. There was no answer, but she didn't worry at first, thinking that they had gone out together. An hour later she called again. Again there was no answer.

She had barely hung up the phone when it began to ring. It was Ned. He wanted to speak to Elaine.

"I thought she was with you," said Mrs. Perdreau, surprised.

"What do you mean? I was at the church tonight, Grandma. Elaine didn't come with me."

"Oh, my, I forgot about your concert this evening. I'm so forgetful these days," she fretted.

"Did she say where she was going?"

"She went out for a walk late this afternoon, and said that if she wasn't back by dark she would be at your house."

"Did you call there?"

"Yes, twice. Nobody's there. She's been gone quite a while."

Ned fell silent. His grandmother asked him where he was calling from.

"I stopped by a friend's house—look, I'm coming home. I don't like the idea of her being out alone like that."

"Do you have any idea where she might be, Ned?"

"I know she likes to walk in the evening..."

After a pause he added, "I bet she went and got that telescope of mine. She's probably outside stargazing. It's a pretty clear night. I'll check at my house first."

Within twenty minutes he was at his grandmother's house. She had turned on all the outside lights, and was waiting for him in the driveway.

Ned wondered if Elaine had perhaps gone for a walk in the woods and lost her way. There was an old path by the small house that she might have taken. He found a flashlight and went outside.

Half an hour later he came out of the woods alone. As he walked by the old house something caught his eye—a light. But when he investigated it turned out to be, as he expected, merely a reflection of his flashlight beam in the glass pane of a window.

He thought of a dilapidated boathouse behind some trees near the marsh. After searching that area, he walked along the edge of the marsh for the length of the yard. At the dock he stopped and called for her again, shining the flashlight along the planks. In momentary apprehension, he let the beam of light fall on the marsh itself, at a part clear of the grasses, where the water was relatively deep. But Ned dismissed the idea before it could even form in his head, expecting to see Elaine returning at any moment. He went back to the house.

Mrs. Perdreau was standing on the back steps under the porch light, waiting for him.

"I just called your house again," she said. "Still no answer."

"I'm going to take the car down the driveway. She might have walked out to the highway, and be on her way back now."

Mrs. Perdreau put her hand on his arm as he was turning to go.

"Maybe she doesn't want to be found, Ned," she suggested reluctantly.

"Why wouldn't she?"

"I don't know, Ned. I found her crying this afternoon, crying her eyes out, and she wouldn't tell me what was wrong. She said it was something personal, and that she would get over it. Maybe she was on the phone and had a fight with a boyfriend—I don't know. Does she have a boyfriend? Do you know why she might have been so upset?"

Ned said he didn't know why she was suddenly distraught.

"She doesn't have a boyfriend as far as I know, Grandma. It must have been something else, but I don't know what. Maybe..."

"Maybe what?"

"Maybe she wasn't as upset as you thought. Are you sure it was that bad?"

"Well, it struck me so at the time...," said Mrs. Perdreau. "It made me want to cry myself to see her like that."

Ned sat down heavily on the steps, wracking his brain for where Elaine might have gone.

"Do you suppose she would have hitchhiked?" asked his grandmother.

"No!" he said instantly, emphatically — but the next moment, he wasn't sure.

"But why would she do that, Grandma? You think she's running away?"

Mrs. Perdreau slowly shook her head in bewilderment. She was noticeably anxious now.

Ned stood up and searched in his pockets for his car keys.

"I think we may be getting a little carried away here," he said nervously, clearing his throat. "I'm going back to check at my house again. If she's not there I'll drive out to the highway."

When he got back to his house he looked around the yards and woods there with the flashlight, calling out for her until his voice became somewhat hoarse, still with the expectation of hearing or seeing her at any moment. He drove back to his grandmother's place, hoping that Elaine would be there by now. It wasn't until he was pulling into the yard that he thought of the motel down the highway.

Mrs. Perdreau came out to the car.

"I thought of somewhere she might have gone," he said. "That little motel down the road."

"Well I don't know whatever for but I suppose it's possible."

He shrugged and sighed, turned the car around, and drove back down the driveway. He moved along the dirt drive slowly, still looking for her along the way. He didn't expect to find Elaine at the motel, yet he couldn't think where else she might be, unless something very bad had happened to her.

He was very worried now, and in his imagination he suddenly saw her walking along the highway and being forced into a car. Such things happened, after all! Images of her in all kinds of trouble and danger went through his mind. Now he even wondered about the possibility of suicide. Had she been lying to him when she told him that she was feeling better, and no longer depressed?

As he turned onto the asphalt road his legs went weak, and one trembled a little as he stepped on the clutch changing gear.

"Please, God, let me find her," he prayed.

At the house Mrs. Perdreau went into Elaine's room and looked around. She checked the closet and the chest-of-drawers, but could not really tell if anything was missing, not knowing exactly how much clothing or other belongings Elaine had brought with her.

She saw a folded piece of paper on the bed table. She opened it with trepidation, but the paper was blank; it was only a bookmark. Deeply concerned, but resisting panic, she went to her favorite chair in the den and sat down to pray.

*   *   *   *   *   *

At the motel, something unexpected had happened to Elaine as she lay in the bed waiting — waiting, and listening to the television set to drown out her own thoughts. She closed her eyes, still listening to the meaningless chatter of commercials and shows, and, within a few minutes, she fell asleep. Within an hour and a half, she was having a dream unlike any other she had ever experienced. It was a dream which, despite its elements of fantasy and illogicality, was as real and vivid as waking life, but even more so because of the intense, overwhelming emotion she felt in it. She woke from it gasping in an exhilaration of terror, like someone experiencing the

141

downward plunge of a roller coaster from dizzying heights. But it wasn't a physical danger which had terrified her.

Elaine dreamed that, for some unknown reason, she had committed murder. She had shot to death a young woman. In the dream, when she realized what she had done, she was horrified— aghast at the enormity of the crime she had committed—and was gripped with a paralyzing, agonizing fear and remorse, a compound of feelings more powerful than any she had ever known. In this state of horror, she slowly awakened, and did not realize for many long moments that she had been asleep. For those long moments she still believed that she had done this awful thing, and she sat up in her bed shaking with emotion.

Gradually, she realized that what she had experienced was a dream, but she still trembled for a long while, taking deep breaths to slow her pounding heart, as it came into her mind with searing certainty, that this was a dream from God.

* * * * * *

Mrs. Perdreau heard the screen porch door creaking open, and knew it wasn't Ned, having heard no car drive up. She hurried through the house and met Elaine at the doorway.

Elaine looked exhausted, breathing hard from having run part of the way. Patches of perspiration showed through her shirt. When she saw her grandmother she lowered her eyes and would hardly look at her as they spoke.

"Where have you been, Elaine?" asked Mrs. Perdreau breathlessly. "We've been worried to death!"

"I'm sorry—I was walking," she said quietly, glancing over at a clock. "I didn't realize how long I'd been gone."

"Ned's out looking for you. He's been searching everywhere for you."

"I'm sorry," she repeated.

Mrs. Perdreau asked her where she had been walking—hadn't she heard Ned calling for her?

"No, I didn't—honestly," Elaine answered wearily, letting her head droop down even farther.

The telephone rang, and Mrs. Perdreau stepped into the kitchen. It was Ned. She told him that Elaine was home now.

Some minutes later he drove up in the yard. His grandmother met him at the back door.

"Where's she been?" he asked, looking relieved, tired, and exasperated.

"Just out walking, she said. She told me she didn't hear you calling."

"Where is she?"

"She's gone to bed. She said she didn't feel well, and didn't want to talk about this anymore tonight."

Ned went to her bedroom door anyway and knocked.

"Can I speak to you a minute, Elaine?"

She came to the door and opened it a little, enough to show her face. Remaining on the other side of the threshold, Ned looked at her for a few moments with a serious, searching expression.

"Are you all right?" he finally asked.

She made an effort to look him in the eye.

"Yes."

"Where were you walking?" he asked curiously, after a pause.

"Down the highway…"

"Towards town?"

"No, the other way."

He began another question, but didn't finish it. Her head had drooped lower and lower, and she looked so weary and drawn that he decided his interrogations could wait.

"Sorry," he murmured.

"I'm sorry," she said, looking up, "that I worried you, and Grandma."

"Okay…but please don't do it again," he begged her with a weary smile.

He received the faintest suggestion of a smile in return.

"I'll try not to."

"I think I'll stay here tonight, in the guest bedroom upstairs."

"Why?"

"I'm so worn out, I don't feel like driving home."

"Oh, okay. Ned, Grandma didn't call my parents, did she?"

"No, I don't think so."

Elaine took a deep breath of relief.

"Please don't tell them about tonight. It would worry them needlessly on their vacation. I was just out walking."

"I won't mention it, Elaine," Ned responded, but he looked at her as though he didn't really believe she had just been out for a walk.

"I'm tired, too," she said. "So I guess I'll say goodnight now."

"Goodnight, Elaine."

She closed the door, and Ned walked away, but didn't go upstairs. He talked with his grandmother a little while, until she went on to bed, turning off most of the downstairs lights on her way. In the den, he sat down on the couch which faced Elaine's bedroom and watched her door. Crossing his arms over his chest, Ned eventually fell in and out of a light doze, but felt certain that if he did fall asleep, he would wake up if she came out of her room.

*   *   *   *   *   *

Elaine was standing by her bed, looking at herself in a murky old mirror which hung on the wall just at eye level. The face she saw there dimly was solemn and exhausted; the mouth was frowning, the eyes swollen and slightly stained with black make-up. And yet those eyes stared back at her with a hesitant, inquiring look for once, and something else indefinable.

Somehow, a gift had been bestowed, and it astonished her. She had never been certain of anything before, but she was now.

She turned off the light and got into bed, thinking of those things which had come to her lately as signs, warnings, and messages of deterrence and even hope. These were things she couldn't deny. Still, it was agonizing to think of an uncertain future, and the struggle that surely lay ahead of her. As she contemplated that vague future, she was flooded with her old pessimism and fear, and wondered if she had made a terrible mistake tonight in not using the gun. She had always been more afraid of life than death—hoping that death was only oblivion—and yet she knew better now.

For a moment, she wished things had not changed, that no signs, no hope had been offered her. She began to weep in bewilderment, until she remembered something, and grew calmer.

"Help me," she whispered aloud.

*   *   *   *   *   *

In the early morning hours before daylight, Elaine woke up in a dark, shadowy room. The air was still and quiet; no sounds of birds or insects, or even the rustle of a breeze broke the stillness and peace. There was a kind of peace inside her, and fearing it might pass, she savored it all the more. In the serenity of the room and the comfort of her bed, she closed her eyes and dozed off while the darkness gradually softened and yielded to the coming day.

When Elaine opened her eyes again, it was as yet more dark than light, but the day was being born. She wrapped herself in a robe and went to the window. Outside, in the eastern sky, the morning star shimmered like a speck of diamond in the twilight of dawn, brilliant as a flare.

About the Author

KAREN STOKES lives in Charleston, South Carolina, where she has worked as a manuscript archivist for over 25 years. A graduate of the College of Charleston and the University of South Carolina, she has authored or edited numerous works of fiction and non-fiction relating to South Carolina history. Carolina Twilight is based on her experiences as a teenager and young adult dealing with depression.

Available From
Green Altar Books

If you enjoyed this book, perhaps some of our other titles will pique your interest. The following titles are now available for your reading pleasure... Enjoy!

Catharine Savage Brosman
An Aesthetic Education and Other Stories

Randall Ivey
A New England Romance & Other SOUTHERN Stories

Suzanne Parfitt Johnson
Maxcy Gregg's Sporting Journal 1842 - 1858

James Everett Kibler
Tiller (Clay Bank County)

Karen Stokes
Belles: A Carolina Romance
Honor in the Dust
The Immortals
The Soldier's Ghost: A Tale of Charleston

Gold-Bug *(Mystery & Suspense Imprint)*
Michael Andrew Grissom
Billie Jo

Brandi Perry
Splintered: A New Orleans Tale

Martin L. Wilson
To Jekyll and Hide

FREE BOOK OFFER

SIGN-UP FOR NEW RELEASE notifications and receive a free downloadable edition of Lies My Teacher Told Me: The True History of the War for Southern Independence & Other Essays by Dr. Clyde N. Wilson by visiting FreeLiesBook.com or by texting the word "Dixie" to 345-345. You can always unsubscribe and keep the book, so you've got nothing to lose!